EMMA AND THE MINOTAUR

2nd Edition

Jon Herrera

CONTENTS

PROLOGUE

The Music in the Forest

A ndrew Milligan was running.

Deep in the shadows of Glenridge Forest, Andrew ran. In his right hand, he held a useless flashlight, drained of power. On his head, his safety helmet jerked up and down with each of his strides and each of his stumbles. Grasping branches pulled at his worn work clothes from all sides like long, withered hands endeavouring to slow him down.

Rumbling footsteps, thundering ever closer, drove Andrew forward.

His memories were a confused patchwork, a mesh of fractured images: a great city reflected in a rear-view mirror, a woman and a boy inside an empty apartment, an old car bathed in dim moonlight, strange music that called to him and begged him to follow.

He could hear the music now as he ran. A sweet,

rich melody drifted to him among the trees. Its source was just ahead, deeper into the forest, promising sanctuary. He could see it now, shimmering silver, undulating in time with the music. He did not know what awaited him ahead, but before him, there was light and music. Behind him, the demon.

Andrew had glimpsed the creature for only a moment. As though waking from a dream, he had found himself in a dark forest, unable to remember how he had arrived there. Thunder had pealed, announcing the creature. The monster had emerged from the darkness, tall and imposing, crowned with horns. It had towered over him. Blazing eyes had bathed the forest crimson.

Andrew had fled.

He threw away the flashlight. He reached up and ripped the helmet off his head. Sharp pain stabbed at his sides. His legs burned. Joints and muscles screamed at him to stop running.

The shimmering light drew closer. Through the trees he could see a circle of light. The moon had come down to the forest to rest. The music and the light pulled him forward. He struggled for breath. Ragged gasps of warm air burned in his throat. The demon's footsteps pushed him onward.

Andrew broke into a clearing. A great, gnarled tree rose at the glade's centre. Nestled beneath its branches, the moon gleamed in the night. Silver tendrils of light reached out to him like long, caressing fingers. They carried with them the sweet melody that had brought him here. He remembered now. It was the music that had drawn him to the forest. It had called to him in the night.

Thunder roared. The monster was near. A growl, like that of an enraged animal, burst out of the darkness.

But he understood now. The music was the light. The light was the music. He rushed into the clearing, to the great tree, and leaped into the moon.

Andrew Milligan fell into another world.

CHAPTER ONE

The Disappearing Boy

E mma Wilkins was eleven years old and lived on Belle Street. Early in the school year, Emma became obsessed with a boy who disappeared. It all began on the first day of class during morning recess.

Emma sat on a swing, swaying her feet in small circles, reading the book that she had smuggled out of her classroom. She was keeping half an eye on some boys who were bouncing a tennis ball off the side of the school building, wary of them because she had been a victim of a stray tennis ball once or twice before.

During one of her glances up from the book, she spotted the disappearing boy quite by accident. He was a plain-looking boy who was trying very hard to be very hard to notice. He roamed around the playground with his hands in his pockets. He stared at the ground and avoided eye contact with the other children. Whenever anyone went near him, he spun in place not-too-subtly and turned the other way, suddenly needing to be somewhere else very urgently. It was clear the boy did not want to make any friends.

Emma decided he was probably a spy, or maybe an explorer from an alien civilization forbidden from making contact with the backward locals. She dogeared the book and jumped down off the swing, intent on making a beeline to the boy.

The school bell tolled, interrupting her plans. A swarm of children rushed past her. She lost sight of the boy in the crowd. She stood on her tiptoes and tried to peek over their heads, but it was to no avail. Even the smallest eighth grader towered over her. She jumped in place and craned her neck, struggling to see over the receding throng.

Several children stopped to stare at her. Her brother stood among them. His expression was equal parts confusion and embarrassment.

"Hey, Emma," Will said. "What are you doing?"

"Nothing," Emma said. "Just looking for some-one."

"Who?"

"A spy," she said.

Will shook his head. He did not seem the least bit surprised that Emma had discovered an alien spy on her very first day at Briardale Middle School. It just had to be some sort of record.

"You better get to class," he said. "You don't want to get in trouble on your first day."

She sighed. Her neck was starting to hurt. Will was probably right.

They entered the school together. Will went straight down the hall to his classroom on the first floor. Emma's class was on the second floor.

She made her way to the stairwell, but instead of rushing up the stairs, she stood at the bottom of the steps like a sentinel, watching as the remaining stragglers ran past her. The boy was not among them.

"Go to class, please," a deep voice said, startling her.

The voice belonged to a tall man with fringes of grey hair on his otherwise bald head. He stood nearby, wiping his glasses with a small, square cloth. The beginnings of a smile turned up the corners of his mouth. Emma had not seen him approach.

"Sorry!" She fled up the stairs. "I was just looking for someone."

To the second floor she went. After a round of peeking into the wrong classrooms, and receiving questioning glances from the wrong teachers, she located the correct one. It was the room containing the young woman tapping away at the floor with her foot. It looked to Emma as though Ms Robins was waiting for something. She hoped it arrived soon.

Emma entered the classroom and immediately stepped back in surprise. The boy she had been looking for sat at the desk nearest the door, hands folded neatly in front of him, eyes pointed forward in rapt attention.

"You're in my class? How did you get here?" she said, more loudly than intended. Plain brown eyes turned to regard her, but he did not say a word.

"Emma!" Ms Robins said. "Sit down! And try not to be late next time!"

"Yes, Ms Robins," Emma said. "Sorry, Ms Robins." She took another quick glance at the boy and then took her seat near the back of the class. She would have to confront the spy at another time, but now she knew where to find him. It would be almost too easy.

When lunchtime came around, the boy disappeared again. The instant the bell tolled, he flew out the door like a wizard on a broomstick. Emma chased after him, but by the time she reached the hall, he had already vanished into thin air.

She would have to find him in the cafeteria.

The lunchroom was noisy, filled to the brim as it was. Laughter erupted now and then from one table or another. Occasionally, an objectionable part of someone's lunch would streak through the air, an event followed by a protesting yelp, or an admonishment from a teacher.

Emma scanned her surroundings as she sipped out of a box of apple juice. She sat at her brother's table. Will's two best friends, both also in grade eight, filled out two other seats. Joey claimed to tolerate her. Kevin claimed not to.

"It's so packed in here this year," Kevin said. "It's

all the stupid grade sixes."

"Yeah," Joey said. "So many new ones." He glanced at Emma, the sixth grader.

"Emma's not that stupid," Kevin said. "Stupid, sure, but not as much as all the other ones."

"Thanks," Emma said, too preoccupied with her task to deal with Kevin's insults at the moment. The boy had to be somewhere in the cafeteria. All she had to do was find him.

But the problem that had presented itself in the playground once again reared its head. There were too many heads in the way. It was a continual problem for Emma, and she could not think of a solution for it that did not involve wearing stilts or carrying around a box or a barrel. Either solution would have suited her just fine, but she was sure there were rules against them. Most fun things, in her experience, were usually outlawed. She would have to think out of the box (or the barrel) this time.

She stood up. Apple juice still in hand, she climbed on top of her chair. A carrot stick flew past her head.

From her new vantage point, she estimated that she could see approximately two-thirds of the students in the cafeteria. But if the boy did not want to be found, he was likely to be somewhere in the outer fringes. She needed to go even higher.

She climbed on top of the table. There was some rattling of lunch trays and soda cans. Kevin protested loudly.

"Emma, what are you doing?" Will said, shaking his head.

"Looking for someone," she said. A pizza crust sailed past her, inches from her face. Three tables over, the boys who had been playing with the tennis ball during recess were now taking aim at her with various bits of their lunch. One of them held an unusually large pickle, turning it in his hand this way and that as though testing its heft. Emma hated pickles, no matter what their size or how well-balanced they were.

"Mr Clarence is coming," Joey said in a hush.

Emma did not take her eyes off the pickle. She was ready to dodge out the way any second now. She did not know who Mr Clarence was. He sounded important, sure, but she really did not want to get walloped by an unusually large pickle, or a pickle of any size, really.

"Emma," Will said. "What are you doing? You're going to get in trouble."

"Oh, fine!" she said. She narrowed her eyes at the pickle-wielder in warning, then turned around to see the tall, grey-haired man from before, the one she had run into at the bottom of the stairs.

"Oh. Hello," she said.

"Emma," Will said. "He's the principal. Mr Clarence."

Emma blinked. "Oh. Hello, sir, Mr Clarence."

"What is your name?" the tall man said.

Emma could not tell if she was in trouble or not. Behind his thick-rimmed glasses, Mr Clarence's eyes had something of a twinkle in them, a slight wrinkling at the corners, as though he was holding back a smile.

"My name is Emma, Mr Clarence."

"Please get down from there, Emma," he said.

"Yes, Mr Clarence," she said.

Before she could comply, an unusually large pickle walloped Emma in the back of the head.

The next morning during attendance, Emma kept her eyes fixed on the boy. She suspected that he was, in fact, a wizard, and that he could make himself disappear whenever he wanted to. But if she paid close attention while Ms Robins called out their names, she could find out his identity, and then she could look him up in a wizard directory, if such a thing existed, at her father's university.

The boy sat in much the same way as he had the day before. He remained perfectly still, hands on his desk, his full attention focused on Ms Robins. His hair was neat. His clothes were clean, though faded. It was all perfectly suspicious, almost magically so.

"Collins, Suzanne," Ms Robins called out. The girl directly behind the boy raised her hand.

"Close!" Emma whispered.

"Cosby, Laura."

"Present!"

"Grieger, Eric."

"Here!"

"Johns, Jeff."

"Present. Here."

"Laurier, Molly."

"Here!"

And so on down the list. But still the boy barely moved.

Ms Robins continued. "Wilkins, Emma," she said.

Silence. No one responded this time. Emma, filled with anticipation, focused more intently on the boy. Maybe this was it.

"Wilkins, Emma!" Ms Robins repeated, exasperated.

Still no one answered. But now the boy moved. He turned his head slowly until he faced the back of the classroom. His plain brown eyes shifted their gaze directly toward Emma. Did he know she was onto him?

Ms Robins stepped swiftly to the side of Emma's desk. "Wilkins, Emma!" she said.

Emma frowned. She realized everyone else in the class was looking at her too. "Collins, Suzanne" was snickering.

"Yes, Ms Robins?" Emma said, confused.

"Are you present, Emma? Do you remember your own name?"

Emma raised her hand and barked a swift "Present!"

"Finally!" Ms Robins said. "Good. So everyone's here, including Emma." She pressed her clipboard to her chest and turned back toward her own desk at the front of the classroom.

"Everyone?" Emma said.

Ms Robins sighed and turned around. "Is there a

problem, Emma?"

"You said everyone's here, Ms Robins, but you never called his name. Can't you see him? Is he invisible?"

"Emma, who and what in the world are you talking about?"

"Him!" Emma said. She surged from her chair and raised her arm, index finger extended, intending to point at the boy. Instead, she punched her own notebook and sent it flying straight into the suddenly astonished face of "Johns, Jeff."

"Emma Wilkins!" Ms Robins said. "Sit down right this minute!" She pointed furiously and repeatedly toward the ground. "That's one strike for disturbing the class!"

Over on the other side of the room, on the wall opposite the door, hung a poster board with the word "STRIKES" written at the top of it. Ms Robins stomped over to her desk and picked up a permanent marker. She then stomped the rest of the way to the poster board and wrote on it:

EMMA WILKENS: X

Being the first one on the Strike Board and the misspelling of her last name both mortified Emma in equal amounts. She opened her mouth to protest, but Ms Robins raised a finger with one hand and, with the other, she lifted the marker up toward the Strike Board again, threatening to write another angry "X" beside Emma's name.

Emma pressed her lips together into a thin line to keep herself from speaking. A strike was not the worst thing in the world. It was slightly less bad than two strikes, but infinitely better than three. She would have to be on her very best behaviour from now on. But at least now she knew the boy was, in fact, a wizard, and it was a near certainty that she was the only one who could see him.

On Wednesday, the boy did not show up to school at all, at least not in any visible manner.

Emma squinted at the empty desk. She focused and held her breath. Maybe if she looked hard enough, she could break through whatever magical barrier the boy was using to shield himself.

After two minutes, she could see many specks of colour floating in the air. The boy was materializing before her eyes. The trick was working, but she was getting dizzy.

She decided to try a different, more tangible approach. She raised her hand.

"Yes?"

"May I go to the bathroom, Ms Robins?"

The teacher nodded hesitantly.

Emma made her way to the front of the classroom and stood next to the boy's desk.

"Are you here?" she whispered. There was no answer. Emma reached out and tried to touch the invisible boy. Her hand passed through the air without resistance. Perhaps he was also intangible while invisible.

"Oh, fine," she said.

"Emma," Ms Robins said suddenly. "Are you going to the bathroom, or are you just going to stand there all day?"

Emma fled the room.

The worst time of day at the Wilkins household, as Emma saw it, was right after dinner because it was the appointed time for violin practise. Albert Einstein had been a physicist. Emma's father was also a physicist. Albert Einstein had played the violin. Emma's father, William, also played the violin. It was a requirement of some sort. Emma often wondered how her father had ever passed his physicist test. He would have been hopeless in the violin section.

Emma sat on the living room floor with her homework spread out on the coffee table in front of her. The screeching from her father's office made it difficult to concentrate. Doing her homework under duress was a daily occurrence. It was tradition. But today, the violin's shrieking was particularly grating.

She put her pencil down and stood up. Her father's office was the first room down the hallway. She knocked on the door.

The screeching halted, and the door swung open.

Her father's office was messy. A wide bookshelf, jammed with physics textbooks and science fiction hardcovers, stood along the wall. Thick reference books littered the floor, scattered among boxes overflowing with scientific papers. More papers still, some of them William's own publications, cluttered his desk in precarious stacks.

"Hey, Dad," Emma said.

"Hey, I was just practising." Her father was thin and tall, almost lanky. Will shared those same physical traits, but, somehow, the height gene had soared past Emma, probably right over her head, missing her entirely.

"I know, Dad," she said. "I could hear you. I just wanted to talk to you."

"What's wrong?"

"Nothing." It was mostly true. She could not very well tell that him he was a terrible violin player, and that she could barely think because of the constant shrieking of his violin. What she hoped for was a break from the screeching for just a little while. She could not think of anything to talk about, but that was a never a problem when she was with her father. Something always popped into his head, and even a physics lesson was better than listening to the screeching violin.

"Emma," he said, sitting down on his chair, "did you catch that wizard you were chasing?"

"No," she said. "No luck. I think he can turn invisible too."

"He must be very powerful." He frowned. "You know," he said, adjusting his glasses as he often did when he was about to relate an important lesson. "If he isn't actually a wizard, then maybe he's going somewhere outside the school when he disappears, don't you think?"

"Maybe. But we're not allowed to leave the school at lunchtime."

"I know," he said, "but just suppose he did. That would explain a lot, wouldn't it?"

"I guess so."

"How many exits are there at Briardale?"

"Three or four, I think," Emma said. "Why?"

Her father smiled. "I'll leave the rest as an exercise to the student."

"Dad!"

It was pointless to argue. Emma would have to puzzle out the rest of it on her own. It was frustrating, but she had more to go on than she did before. Her father was vague but helpful. He would hint at an answer but never give it to her outright.

Emma sighed. "Thank you," she said. She hugged him and then went back to her spot at the coffee table to continue her homework and mull over her new puzzle.

The screeching resumed.

Despite the shrieking from her father's office, it did not take long for Emma to figure out what he had been implying. She found out from Will that there were four ways in and out of Briardale Middle School. There were the main doors at the front of the building, the big doors leading to the playground in the back, and two smaller side doors. If the boy left the school during lunchtime, he had to go through one of those exits. If he always left through the same door, all Emma had to do was wait for him at the correct one. If she waited at a different door each time, it would take four tries, at most, to catch him.

But Emma narrowed her options even further. She did not think the boy would leave through the main doors because they were the main doors and thus not good for sneaking. The back doors were also out of the question because a teacher always supervised them whenever the students were let out. The only possibilities that remained were the two side doors, meaning that Emma had a fifty percent chance of catching the boy on her very first try.

There was a small problem she had to overcome. The boy, because he sat so close to the classroom door, was always prepared for a quick exit. She would have to figure out a way to sneak out of the room before he did.

It was twenty minutes before lunchtime. Emma raised her hand.

"Emma," Ms Robins said.

"May I go to the bathroom, please?"

Emma had decided that if she delayed too long, Ms Robins would make her wait until the end of class. Twenty minutes seemed just about right.

"Can't you wait till lunch?"

"Sorry, Ms Robins," Emma said, doing her best to sound desperate. "I really can't."

The teacher glanced at the clock on the wall. She pursed her lips for a moment. "Go ahead," she said, eventually, with what appeared to be considerable effort.

Emma rushed out the door, casting a sideways glance at the disappearing boy on her way out. Her heart raced as she sprinted down the stairs and to the first floor of the school. She peeked to either side of the hall and found it empty. There were no skulks about except for her.

She tiptoed toward the far door. Ten feet down the hall, she decided that tiptoeing was far too slow and resumed walking normally. Twenty feet down, she crouched beside an open door and listened to a lesson about unit conversion and the metric system. A little over nine metres down the hall, she stopped to take a drink from a water fountain.

She made it out the door without incident. She looked up at the sky to determine the time. The sun stood roughly straight up above her head so it was close to noon. She could not figure out how to tell the minutes.

With a sigh, she made her way to the side of the building, just beyond the wall, and crouched, peeking around the corner, a hunter waiting for her prey.

Some unknown minutes later, according to Emma's estimate based on the position of the sun, the school bell declared it was finally time for lunch.

Momentarily, the door creaked open and out came the wizard boy. He stuck his head out and peered around like a mouse looking out for cats. Emma resisted the urge to pounce on him right then, suddenly curious about where he went during lunchtime. Perhaps he had a secret lair.

Confident there were no cats about, the boy darted out the door and started running.

Emma waited until he was a good distance away, then chased after him. The boy ran past the playground, raced across the soccer field, and dashed beyond the school grounds into the surrounding neighbourhood.

The boy slowed to a walk, strolling down the sidewalk with purpose, but with less urgency than before. He turned his head to look around. Emma ducked behind a tree.

She stalked him all the way to a park, hiding now and then behind bushes and the occasional fire hydrant. The street was quiet, but a driver or two slowed to cast curious glances her way.

At the park, the boy ignored the dirt footpath that wound through a cluster of picnic benches. Instead, he stepped onto the grass, cut across the field, and marched all the way to an unwelcoming thicket beyond. A dense group of lanky trees grew there among a mantle of short, drab brush.

The boy disappeared under the shade of the trees. Emma followed slowly, cautious of magical traps.

The air inside the thicket was cool and smelled of moss. A creek, little more than a trickle of water, followed a winding course among the trees. The boy was nowhere to be seen.

"Open Sesame!" Emma said. Nothing happened. "Abracadabra? Alakazam?" She sighed, disappointed in her limited knowledge of words of power.

She considered hiding in the brush to wait for the boy to return, but then she noticed a curious log bridging the banks of the creek. The log was old and rotted, so it was almost certainly magical. Beyond the log stood a steep little hill. It was nearly vertical, but there were lots of roots and stones sticking out of it. The boy had probably levitated over it.

Emma stepped gingerly across the old log, careful not to slip on its mossy surface.

The climb up the slope gave her difficulty. Halfway up, she looked back down and decided the hill was, in actual fact, a cliff. Nevertheless, despite several scrapes, she made it all the way to the top, past whatever magical defences the boy had conjured up.

She took a deep breath and smiled in triumph, ready for whatever wondrous sight awaited her.

A loud pop interrupted her celebration. She looked down. The slope was much gentler on this side of the hill, levelling off gradually into a small glade. A paltry waterfall springing from a rocky ridge fed the creek, widening it into a small rivulet.

A big, flat rock stood at the centre of the glade. The boy sat upon it, drinking from a can of soda.

It looked like a normal can of soda. A regular root beer. Not at all magical.

"Hey, boy!" Emma called down. "Are you a wizard?"

The boy, startled, almost fell off the rock.

"A wizard?" he said, looking up. "I'm Jake."

Emma frowned. "Jake" was not a wizardly name. "Jake?" she said.

"Jake," the boy said. He stood up on the big rock, glanced around nervously, and wiped his hand on his jeans.

"Jake? What Jake?" Emma said. There was still a chance he was a spy, or an alien explorer, or even a time traveller. "Jake who?"

"I'm Jake Milligan," he said.

CHAPTER TWO

Wizard Falls

E mma slid down the slope. She approached the boy cautiously, wary of tricks, magical or extraterrestrial in nature.

"Hi, Jake," she said, eyes narrowing in suspicion. "I'm Emma Wilkins."

"I know," Jake said. He crouched and packed his things into an old backpack. It was too small for him. There were several holes in it. Emma could see that the biggest tear had already been mended, but now the mending was coming apart. The boy's jeans had been patched on one side at the knee.

"Why do you come here?" Emma said. "You know we're not allowed to leave the school."

Jake shrugged. He jumped off the rock and started for the hill, kicking the now empty can of soda into the rivulet.

Emma circled around and intercepted him, placing herself directly in his path. He did not slow down.

"Where are you going?" she said, walking backward.

"Back to school," Jake said.

"But why? I've been trying to catch you for ages!"

"I know," he said. "I've seen you."

Emma stumbled, surprised by the change in elevation behind her. They had reached the foot of the hill. In that instant, she envisioned herself falling toward Jake. He would catch her, and then, surely, he would stop walking and would talk to her.

She twisted expertly and changed the direction of her stumble. Jake twisted expertly and dodged right around her.

She landed hard on the ground. The boy stopped walking then and, for a moment, Emma thought he would reach down and help her get up. Instead, he shook his head.

"I don't want any friends," he said. He walked on up the hill.

She stood up with a groan. The fall added several more scrapes to the day's tally. Two splinters the size of small branches stuck out of her right index finger. She winced and moaned as she pulled them out one by one, watching thin trickles of blood roll down her skin. She put her finger in her mouth and looked up the hill. Jake was nowhere to be seen.

Emma limped her way back to school. The long walk gave her time to realize there were several things she had not considered before, mainly anything to do with consequences and repercussions. Now that she had time to think about it, her father would never suggest that she leave class early. In fact, he would be decidedly against it. Then there was Ms Robins, who did not appear to be the forgiving type. Emma was probably in for a long lecture upon her return, and maybe even imprisonment in the school dungeon. Her best hope was that Ms Robins had simply forgotten the whole thing. It was possible, she thought, since the teacher was a very busy person with lots of things in her mind like lesson plans and marking. It would be perfectly reasonable for her to forget something as insignificant as one student disappearing for almost an hour and returning to school covered in scratches and bruises.

Her hopes were dashed as soon as she came within sight of the school. Ms Robins stood outside, arms in the air, gesturing spiritedly. She was yelling at poor Will.

Emma approached. Will shook his head. Ms Robins stopped yelling and started tapping her foot. The teacher glanced at her watch impatiently as Emma limped toward them.

"Emma Wilkins!" Ms Robins said as soon as Emma was close enough. She crossed her arms. "What do have to say for yourself?"

Emma opened her mouth to speak, but then closed it again. Ms Robins had only paused for breath.

"What do you think you're doing disappearing like that? You've been gone since before lunch! I was worried sick, and I thought I had lost a student. You come with me right now." She stomped away toward the school. Emma limped behind her as quickly as she could manage. "You are in serious trouble, Emma Wilkins. It's only the first week of school, and you are already the most troublesome student I've ever had. I can't even think of a suitable punishment for you."

The tirade continued all the way to the classroom where, immediately upon arriving, Ms Robins made a beeline to the Strike Board.

EMMA WILKENS: XX

"Go to your seat and stay there quietly for the rest of lunch," Ms Robins said. "I will write a note about your behaviour. Return it to me, signed by a parent, first thing tomorrow morning!"

On Thursday nights, Emma's father taught a class from seven to ten. As was often the case when he lectured in the evening, he had not come home for dinner.

It had started to rain just after Emma and Will had arrived at the house. It was now six o'clock. The rain had not relented.

Will filled a plate with the previous day's ham and asparagus and took it to his bedroom. Emma did not feel like eating. Instead, she sat on the windowsill in the living room and watched the falling raindrops as they splashed into potholes.

The day had gone very wrong. The wizard boy wanted nothing to do with her. She was scraped and bruised all over. She had two strikes at school. Worst of all, she had to give her father the note from Ms Robins. He would not be happy about that, and on days like today, Emma always relied on him to help lift her spirits. To top it all off, it was raining. The rain always brought a touch of sadness with it she could not explain. It made her feel hollow somewhere inside her chest, like something was missing.

Emma checked the clock on the wall and made a decision. She went to the closet beside the front door and put on a raincoat and a pair of boots. A flashlight hung from a nail on the wall. She grabbed it and put it into one of the coat's oversize pockets.

She opened the front door and went out onto the street. For a moment she stood in place, looking up to the sky, feeling the cool raindrops as they landed on her cheeks. She decided that being out in the rain was a little bit better than sitting inside the house watching it.

With a sigh, she started on her way.

There were many puddles and potholes on Belle Street. Emma jumped joylessly into most of them as she tramped down to Lockhart Road.

To get to the University of Saint Martin, Emma

could walk down to Glendale Avenue and then turn right, straight up The Hill. But the journey would be shorter if she crossed the street and cut through the forest, which spread out in both directions along Lockhart Road.

She was not allowed in the woods after dark, but she had the flashlight with her. She approached the edge of the forest and took it out of her pocket. Glistening, wet boles reflected light back at her as she peered into the darkness. She stood still for a moment and listened to the whisper of the wind and the dripping of the rain, pointing her flashlight around, scanning for danger. When she was satisfied that it was perfectly safe, Emma stepped forward into the forest.

There was a path that led straight to the University of Saint Martin. If Emma walked in a northerly direction, she would run into it eventually. It was just a matter of not getting turned around in the darkness. Luckily, she had her flashlight with her to guide the way. She gave it an appreciative squeeze.

The flashlight blinked off and on.

"Better not do that again," she said.

Emma trudged on. The trees provided some cover from the rain, but there were still plenty of puddles here and there for her to jump into. She slogged through the muddy forest.

An owl hooted from the darkness ahead. Squinting into the night, she turned her head this way and that. The hoot had been faint. She had barely heard it over the sound of the raindrops chattering on the leaves of the trees.

Emma hooted. She waited for a response from the owl.

Something seemed to answer her call, but it was not an owl. It sounded like a musical instrument. Something like a violin, but beautiful, not like the screeching she was used to hearing from her father's office. She took several steps forward and gave her head a vigorous shake to make sure she was not imagining it. The music persisted. She had expected no one to be out and about in this downpour, much less playing the violin in a dark forest. Perhaps it was a very committed physicist.

The music sounded as though it originated from far away, deep in the forest, somewhere off to the right from the direction she was heading. She knew it was not a good idea to take a detour in the dark and risk missing the path to the university, but the music was too wonderful. Its source was too good a mystery to pass up. Besides, she had her flashlight with her to show the way. She tightened her grip on it.

The flashlight blinked off. This time, it did not turn back on. She shook it vigorously to no avail. She tapped the back end of it with her palm as she had seen grownups do. It did not work. The world remained pitch black under the cover of the trees.

The music ceased abruptly.

From the darkness ahead, she heard movement, a violent rustle of leaves among the pattering of the rain. She tapped at the flashlight again, but still it refused to work.

"Deer?" she said. Perhaps it had been a deer and not a bear, or a dragon, or worse.

The leaves rustled again, closer to her this time. Emma backed away from the sound, feeling her way behind her with her foot. She wanted to turn around and run, but she was afraid of running headfirst into a tree.

She tapped the flashlight again. "Please," she said, uttering the only word of power she could remember.

The flashlight came to life, illuminating Emma's surroundings.

Some distance away from her, among the brush, stood a tall figure cloaked in shadow. A pair of horns protruded from the figure's head.

Emma turned and ran, suddenly not caring if she crashed into a tree. Leaves slapped at her face. The undergrowth pulled at her jeans. She slipped and slid all the while as the forest flew by around her. She did not dare look back.

Her mad dash eventually brought her to the edge of the forest. She saw the light of a street lamp, but did not see the rotten branch across her way. She tripped and tumbled forward. Her momentum carried her out onto the road, where she landed hard on hands and knees. The flashlight broke apart, and the batteries flew away.

Breathless, Emma scrambled around to face the woods. Her heart pounded. She stared back in the direction she had come.

The wind howled among the trees, but no monsters came running out.

"Okay," Emma said between ragged breaths. "That was dumb. It was probably a stupid deer."

She crawled to the side of the road and sat down. Her jeans were torn. Her hands and knees were bleeding. She sighed and let the rain wash the blood away. She considered returning home and crawling into bed, but she needed to get her note signed. She needed her father.

Emma stood up and turned down the road toward The Hill. The wind and the rain beat at her face and pulled at her coat. She walked alongside the forest. Soon, the trees gave way to several houses that huddled together between Glenridge Forest and Glendale Avenue. Past the houses she went, and then on up The Hill, called so because of the steep incline of the road there.

The walk up The Hill was slow. Exhausted, in pain, and half-blinded by the rain, she held on to the railing that separated the road from the clumps of trees that grew on the other side of it. A few cars passed her by in both directions, but otherwise the street was fittingly desolate for the harsh weather.

At the top of The Hill, the ground levelled off, and there began the collection of buildings that made up the University of Saint Martin. It was a small university and, typical for that time of night, the complex was mostly deserted except for the few students attending evening classes.

Emma hobbled into the school grounds and entered the mathematics building. She left a trail of water as she made her way to the second floor and into the Physics Department.

When she reached the office of Dr William Wilkins, she found his door shut. She tried to open it. It was locked. She knocked. There was no answer.

"Class time," she said, sighing and slumping her shoulders.

She leaned back against the door and slid down to the floor. A puddle of water formed beneath her. She closed her eyes.

Emma woke up.

She blinked at her father, who held her in his arms. They were inside his office, on his big chair. It took her a moment to realize that she had fallen asleep and, after his class, he must have found her on the floor outside his door and brought her in.

She yawned and snuggled into him. He held her for a while.

"Dad," Emma said, not looking up.

"Yes, dear?"

"I caught the wizard boy."

"Oh? And what happened?"

"He didn't want to be my friend," she said.

"I'm sorry, Emma."

"It's okay. I know why. I realized something."

"What's that?"

"He's very sad," Emma said.

The following day, Emma stayed home from school.

She still did not know how much trouble she was in. During the drive home from the university, Emma had told her father everything. She had told him all that had happened at the school, and all about how she had tried to cut through the forest after dark. He had sent her straight to bed, saying that they would talk about it later. At least he had signed the note from Ms Robins.

When she woke up, Will and her father had already left. The bandages that had been on her knees during the night had fallen off. Her sheets had little stains of blood on them. She gathered them up and threw them in the hamper, wincing at the pain in her hands. They also had small cuts all over them.

Emma showered, got dressed, then went into the kitchen to make herself a slice of toast with peanut butter. A note rested on the counter. It read: "Rest! We will talk tonight." She took the note and put it into her pocket.

After her small breakfast, she went back to her room and pulled an old, yellow lunch box out from under her bed. Inside, among other odds and ends, there was a small fortune in bills and coins. She took some of the money and put it into her other pocket.

She left the house.

Emma walked to the end of the Belle Street and onto Lockhart Road. Following the same route she had taken the night before, after her adventure in the forest, she arrived once again at the intersection of Lockhart and Glendale. This time, instead of turning up The Hill, she crossed the street and made her way to a bus stop.

A girl stood inside the bus shelter. The bright pink headphones on her head stood out against her dark hair. Equally dark were her long sleeve shirt and her jeans. She looked to be a few years older than Emma, so she was probably a university student.

Emma went inside the shelter. The older girl watched her from the moment she arrived until she sat on the bench.

Emma waved.

The girl lowered the headphones to her neck. "Hey, don't I know you?" she said.

"I don't think so," Emma said.

"Are you sure? My name's Lucy. What's yours?"

"Emma," Emma said.

"Emma. You seem familiar, Emma. Emma what?"

"Emma who," said Emma.

"What?"

"Never mind. My name is Emma Wilkins."

Lucy's eyes lit up. "You must be Professor Wilkins's daughter. That's where I've seen you. Did you come by the university during orientation?"

"Yeah, for a little," Emma said. "And that's my

dad."

"I'm in his physics class," Lucy said. "Nice to meet you, Emma."

"Nice to meet you, Lucy."

The squeal of brakes interrupted their conversation. Emma's bus had arrived. It turned out that Lucy was headed to the same destination, so they boarded and sat down together.

"Hey," Lucy said, "aren't you supposed to be at school?"

"Nope," Emma said. "Aren't you?"

"Nope. I don't have class till later. Introduction to Physics, actually, with your dad."

"What a coincidence," Emma said.

When they arrived at Penhurst Mall, Emma followed Lucy from store to store. They wandered around with no real purpose at first. The mall was mostly deserted, though at one point they stumbled upon a small group of elderly men gathered around a giant chess set. They stood close by and watched.

"Are you looking for anything in particular?" Lucy said when they had moved on.

"I'm looking for bait," Emma said. She took a look around. There was a store directory nearby. She stepped up to it and read through the listings.

"Here," she said, putting her finger on the map.

"Luggage?"

Emma nodded. She led the way to the store, and they went inside.

After Emma completed her purchase, they wandered around the mall a little while longer, but it was soon time for them both to go. Lucy had class. Emma had a secret mission.

They sat on a bench outside one of the mall's entrances until Lucy's bus pulled up to the stop.

"I'll see you around," Lucy said.

"Bye!" Emma said.

The older girl left. Emma sat by herself, swinging her feet and enjoying the sun on her face. She clutched the bait to her chest as she waited for her own bus to arrive.

Wizard Falls, as Emma had named it, was bright with sunshine. The light glinted off the slick, wet rocks scattered about the creek. Faint rainbows floated in the air where the trickle of water from the rocky ridge hit a protruding rock and gave off a spray.

Emma was hiding behind a tree, waiting. She was on the far bank across the water from the big rock in the middle of the glade, counting the seconds until her prey appeared. She had set her trap.

She held her breath when she spied the boy coming over the hill.

Jake ambled down the slope and started on his way toward the rock. When he saw the bait, he stopped in his tracks. His eyes darted around. He turned in place, scanning all over the glade for intruders.

It took a few moments for him to appear satisfied

that he was alone. Emma was sure he had not seen her.

Jake moved on toward the rock. A brand new backpack rested on it. It was black and blue, and just about the right size for a boy of eleven.

He stared at the backpack for a moment before picking up the envelope that Emma had placed on top of it. On the envelope she had written the words "For Jake." He turned it this way and that before opening it. Inside, Emma had placed a square, blue card with a single word written in the middle of it:

"Magic."

The boy frowned at the card and turned it over and around just as he had done with the envelope. He placed the card on the rock and sat down next to it. He took out a sandwich from his old backpack and started to eat, staring at the new backpack the entire time.

Emma watched and waited.

When Jake finished eating, he picked up the old backpack and turned it upside down. Its contents spilt out onto the rock. He took one last look around, and then he stuffed his belongings into the new backpack.

Emma envisioned a giant box above Jake's head. She pulled an imaginary string, and the box fell down on the boy and trapped him.

"Okay, crazy girl," Jake said. "You can come out now."

"What?" Emma shouted from behind her hiding

place. She stepped out from around the tree. "You knew I was here?"

"I saw you," Jake said. "Anyway, who else would leave this here?"

"Yeah, I guess," Emma said. She made her way back across the creek. Jake watched her hop from rock to rock, holding her arms out to the sides to keep her balance.

"This isn't how the plan was supposed to go," she said.

"How was it supposed to go?"

"You weren't supposed to know it was me," she said. "You were supposed to think it was a magic backpack from a magic school or something. Wizardry."

"That's insane," he said. "And then what?"

She jumped onto the bank of the creek. "And then… I don't know. I guess you were supposed to say something like, 'Oh no, they have found me,' and then I would know that you know about secret magic schools."

"You really are crazy," he said. "Do you really believe all that stuff?"

Emma felt the colour rise in her cheeks. She looked away. "I guess not," she said. "I guess I don't. Not really. I guess the truth is I just want to be your friend."

He shook his head as though he did not understand. "Why?"

"I don't know," she said. "No reason, I guess. I just saw you all alone one day."

He frowned, annoyed. "You're all alone too," he said. His sharp tone implied he had meant that as an insult.

But Emma nodded vigorously. "I know!" she said. "Exactly!"

He looked from Emma to the backpack. Suddenly, he seemed far away, lost in thought. For a moment, the only sound in the glade was the trickling of the meagre waterfall.

He sighed then looked back to her and gave her a halfhearted smile. "So it's you who needs a friend," he said. "Okay. I'll be your friend, even if you are crazy."

Emma smiled. Immediately, she jumped up on the rock to sit next to Jake. "So Jake," she said, "why are you so sad and angry?"

Jake turned his head toward her and frowned. Emma regretted having opened her mouth without thinking. She expected the boy to jump off the rock and stomp away, but he only shook his head.

"I guess we're friends now so you can say stupid stuff like that."

He stood up but did not stomp away.

"My dad went missing," he said. "We just moved here. I don't know anyone, and my dad is gone. I didn't want to talk to anyone."

"What happened to him?"

"No one knows. He was working one day at the construction site and they said he heard music in the forest. He didn't come home that night."

Emma nodded. "I heard music in the forest too,"

she said. "My dad said it was just my imagination. He says I have a good one. I also thought I saw a man with horns. Got really scared, but it was probably just a deer."

Jake jumped off the rock and went to the edge of the water. He picked up a few pebbles and tried to skip them. Most of his throws went straight in and sank to the bottom. After several attempts, he flung the rest of the pebbles at the rocky ridge. He came back to the rock, wiping his hands on his jeans.

"What kind of music did you hear?" he said. "Do you think you could find where it came from?"

"I don't know. It was like some stuff my dad tries to play, except it was good. I've been thinking maybe it was a singing tree, but that's crazy, right? It was probably just my imagination, like my dad says."

"But what if it's not your imagination?" Jake said. "Maybe it's a mystery, or a puzzle."

A sudden rush of excitement ran through her. She loved a good mystery. Many of her favourite stories had mysteries in them. "Do you really think so?"

"Yeah, probably," Jake said. "So help me solve it?"

"Sure! I think that's a good idea!" She pursed her lips. "I can't really do anything today though. I'm not supposed to even be here. I'm supposed to be home resting, but I'll start thinking of a plan. You have to go back to school, anyway."

Jake nodded. He picked up the new backpack.

"I can't really keep it," he said.

"You put your stuff in it already."

"I was just testing it."

"You have to keep it now," Emma said. "You can't give presents back."

"Fine," he said, "but I'll get you back."

He turned toward the hill. They set out on their way and clambered up and over it.

"Wait a minute," Emma said. "Why isn't your name called during attendance?"

"Oh," Jake said. "The teacher said I'm not on the attendance sheet yet because I registered late. She said they print them every week."

"Oh," Emma said, somewhat disappointed in the solution to that particular mystery.

When Emma returned home, she went directly to her room and put the money that she had left over back into the yellow lunch box. She also put the note from her father in there. It was her custom to keep all her correspondence.

She spent the rest of the afternoon sitting by the coffee table, filling out workbooks for school. She felt bad about having missed a day and did not want to fall behind. Emma had no idea what homework had been assigned for the weekend, so she worked ahead as far as she could.

When her father walked through the door, she stood up to greet him. Her smile faded as soon as she saw the look on his face, suddenly remembering that they were supposed to talk about how much trouble she was in.

"I need to talk to you," he said.

Dejected, she walked over to the kitchen table, pulled back a chair, and sat down. Her father sat across from her.

"Emma," he said. "One of my students talked to me today before class. She was very excited about having met you."

"Lucy," Emma blurted out. This was worse than she thought.

"Yes," he said. "Lucy Leroux. She said that she met you at the bus stop, and that the two of you spent the morning at the mall. I told her she had to be mistaken because you were supposed to be home resting all day."

"Snitch!" Emma said in a whisper. "I'm sorry, Dad. I wasn't thinking."

"You agreed last night that you would rest, Emma. I didn't let you stay home from school so you could go riding buses around town. Didn't you see my note? Whatever were you doing, anyway?"

There was nothing Emma could do, and no excuse she could think of.

"I caught the boy," she said and explained her trap. She told him about Jake Milligan and his missing father, and about how she had agreed to help him find the singing tree.

"Absolutely not," he said. "I forbid it. I don't want you going anywhere near that forest anymore, Emma. There has been another disappearance besides Andrew Milligan. Another construction worker. Something is happening on that construction site down the road, and I want you to stay away from it and away from the forest."

Emma did not argue because she did not know what to say, and because she knew that her father was right. The smart thing to do would be to stay away from the forest.

He continued. "You've always been so good, Emma. I don't know what has happened these last couple of days, but you know what you've done wrong. Let's try to learn from this and not let it happen again. Consider yourself grounded until further notice. Understand?"

"Yes, Dad. I'm sorry, Dad."

He pushed his chair back and stood up.

"Dad," Emma said. "Who else went missing?"

"It was in today's paper," he said. He picked up the newspaper from the kitchen counter and handed it to her.

The Saint Martin Guardian had a front-page article about two missing construction workers: Andrew Milligan and, now, Steven Marks. The article explained that Paigely Builders had hired security guards to patrol the construction site day and night, and that they were doing all they could to help the families of the men who were missing.

Emma's grounding lasted only for the weekend (she was released on good behaviour), but the ban from the forest was in place indefinitely. This would complicate things, but she had made a promise to her new friend, and she was not about to let him down.

CHAPTER THREE

Dinner and a Conspiracy

"**M**atter has mass and occupies space," Emma said.

"Good, Emma," Ms Robins said, somehow draining all the encouragement out of the words.

It was Monday, and the lesson was about matter and energy. Emma had been answering a lot of questions because she had worked far ahead during the weekend. She hoped to change her teacher's opinion about her and maybe even erase her strikes, if such a thing was possible. Emma had brought in two notes that morning: the mean one from Ms Robins, signed by her father, and another excusing her for missing school on Friday. The teacher had accepted them without a word. She had only skimmed over them before throwing them in the trash can. Emma had slipped quietly to her desk, determined to become the perfect student from then on.

At lunchtime, Emma and Jake sneaked away to Wizard Falls. There was enough room on the big rock for the both of them. They sat on top of it under the sunlight. The *drip-drip-drip* of the trickling waterfall provided a backdrop to their conversation.

"How did you find this place?" Emma said.

"I just walked down the road trying to get away from the school," Jake said. "I found it by accident."

"But why did you leave the school?"

Jake took a bite of his sandwich before answering. "Some kids made fun of me on the first day. I didn't feel like being there."

Emma took out an apple and a banana from her backpack.

"You want one, Jake?"

He considered his options and nodded toward the banana.

"Why would kids make fun of you?" Emma said. "You're just a plain, average boy."

"Thanks," he said and pushed her gently on the shoulder. She almost tumbled off the rock. "They made fun of my backpack and my clothes."

"Oh," she said. A quick glance over him revealed he wore the same patched jeans he had worn on Thursday. His shirt had a faded yellow colour, and it was a little too tight for him. His shoes were clean but worn down in places.

They ate in silence until Jake jumped off the rock and stood to face her.

"Emma," he said. "When can we go searching in the forest?"

"Well," she said, "there's a problem."

"What do you mean?"

"My dad won't let me go into the forest now. But that doesn't mean I won't help you find the singing tree. I came up with a plan. It's got two phases: Phase A and Phase B."

Jake frowned. "What's phase one?"

"Phase A," Emma corrected him. "Phase A is you come over to my house on Saturday for dinner. My dad wants to meet you."

"Oh. Then what's phase two?"

"Phase B," Emma said. "Phase B is a secret and I can't tell you it until Phase A and Phase A, Section B are complete."

"There's a Section B now?"

Emma nodded. "It's a part of Phase A, so I didn't mention it before. But part of Phase B happens before Phase A is over, so I had to split it into sections."

"Sounds complicated," Jake said.

"Took me all weekend to figure it out."

Jake shook his head. "But why don't we have one phase and just go into the forest?"

"Because I'm not allowed to go to the forest," Emma said. "You'll like my plan. I just know it. It's better than walking around the forest, anyway. All you have to do is come over to my house on Saturday and then I'll tell you Phase B."

"What about Section B?"

"Phase A, Section B is you have to sleep over."

Saturday afternoon came around, and Emma sat on the windowsill to wait for Jake to arrive. She had her favourite book with her. It was an old copy, worn at the spine, with pages threatening to fall out.

She sat reading her book until nearly five o'clock when she spied the boy and his mother coming down the street. Mrs Milligan was only slightly taller than Jake. She was dressed in what Emma assumed to be her work uniform, and she carried a sizable red purse on her arm. She was speaking to the boy as they walked. Jake only faced forward and nodded from time to time.

Emma waved from the window and ran to open the door. They did not see her until they were at the foot of the driveway. Mrs Milligan smiled at her. The visitors made their way to the front steps.

"Hello, Mrs Milligan," Emma said.

"Call me Vicky," Mrs Milligan said. "It's nice to meet you, Emma. Thank you for the backpack. I can't believe you did that. I told Jake he shouldn't have accepted it, but the boy has no shame. Don't worry, we'll pay you back for it. Actually, since we're here now, I can get you the money right this minute. Let me look through my purse here. I'm sure my wallet's in here somewhere. Now, where could it have gone?"

"Oh, no," Emma said. "Please, don't worry about

it, Mrs Vicky."

"Vicky," she said. "Just Vicky. But really, you must let me pay you back. We appreciate it, of course. If only I could find my darned wallet. It's always going missing, Emma. Ah, here it is. Now, let me just check in here. How much was the backpack, Emma?"

Emma could not remember. "I can't remember," she said.

"Sure you can," Mrs Milligan said, drawing breath. Before she could speak, a shriek from inside the house interrupted her. "What in the world is that?"

"Oh, it's violin practise," Emma said. "But don't worry, my dad is almost done for the day."

"That was a violin?"

"I think so, Mrs Milligan."

"Vicky, Emma. Call me Vicky. What a nice, polite girl you are. I'm glad Jake finally made such a nice friend. He didn't keep the best company back home. They were a bunch of troublemakers, really. I was afraid they would have a bad influence on him."

"Mom!" Jake protested, speaking up for the first time.

"Sorry, kid," she said. "But it's true."

"They were my friends," he said.

"Well, now you have Emma here and I'm glad for it."

Emma blushed. "Thank you, Mrs Milligan," she said.

"Vicky," Mrs Milligan said.

A final, long wail from inside the house announced the end of violin practise. They heard a door open and shut before William Wilkins emerged from the hallway.

"Good afternoon," he said. "You must be Mrs Milligan."

"Call me Vicky, please."

"It's nice to meet you, Vicky," he said. "Will you be joining us for dinner?"

"I'm afraid I can't," she said. "I'm actually on my way to work. Closing shift tonight. I just wanted to see this little one get here safe, and I wanted to meet you and Emma. That's a nice girl you have here. She's so kind and polite. I'm glad Jake made such a good friend."

As the adults exchanged pleasantries, Emma grabbed Jake by the hand and dragged him inside the house. She took him through the living room, past the kitchen, and into the hallway.

"Bathroom's over there," she said. "This is my room here. It's the little one."

"It's bigger than mine," he said. "What's all this stuff?"

Papers and markers littered the bed.

"This is Plan One, Phase B. I can tell you all about it now."

"Wait, there's a Plan A now? Is there a Plan B?"

"There is Plan One and Plan Two. Plan Two is the nuclear option. We won't do that one unless there is an emergency. We can't even talk about it."

Jake rolled his eyes.

"Let me tell you Plan One, Phase B!" Emma continued. "I'm sure you'll love it." She dragged him close to the bed and started shifting papers around. Each sheet had either a drawing or some writing on it. The corner of every piece of paper had a title. One read "Plan One, Phase A, Section B, Draft 6," and the rest all had similar headings. She found the one she was looking for and held it up for him.

"Here!" she said. "Phase B!"

Emma had split the page into three panels. The top panel showed a rectangular building with "Dollar Store" written on it. The middle panel depicted a camera and a kite, with a red arrow pointing from one to the other. The final panel was a drawing of a dozen trees. A kite soared above them.

Jake frowned. "You want us to go to the dollar store and buy a kite and a camera?"

Emma nodded. "Yes," she said, grinning. "And then we tape the camera to the kite and fly it over the forest to take pictures. That way I don't have to go in the forest but we can find the singing tree or even your dad!"

Jake was shaking his head. His face had turned sombre. "That will never work, Emma. Did you really think it would?"

Emma's grin disappeared. "Why not?"

"Have you ever flown a kite before? It will be too heavy with a camera. And how would we push the button?"

Emma sat down on the bed, frowning. She had never flown a kite. She had not thought about how to push the button.

"Hey," Jake said. "I'm sorry. It's a good plan if we could work out the problems. But it'll take too long to take pictures of the whole forest. I think we just need to go in there and search."

"I can't," Emma said. "I'm not allowed."

"I know." He sighed. "I can go alone. I just need you to tell me which way to go."

Emma shook her head. "You shouldn't go alone, Jake. It might be dangerous in there. Two people have disappeared."

"I know," he said, "and one of them is my dad. I have to find him, and I'm going into the forest even if you don't tell me which way to go."

Emma took a deep breath and closed her eyes. "I'll go with you," she said.

"Really?"

"Yeah" she said. "That's Plan Two, after all."

Jake woke up in the middle of the night, disoriented. He did not know where he was.

He pulled a blanket aside and stood up. Light from the street flowed in through a large window, illuminating his surroundings. He had been sleeping on a couch in someone's living room. A clock on the wall showed it was a little past midnight. Opposite the window, a long counter separated the living room from a kitchen.

He had been having nightmares. A thin layer of sweat covered his skin. His shirt was damp. He was thirsty.

He made his way to the kitchen and opened the cupboards until he found the one where the glasses were kept. While pouring himself water, he noticed that the window above the sink was open. The noises of the night drifted inside the house along with a voice he recognized.

Jake suddenly remembered where he was. It was the Wilkinses' house. He had dined with them earlier and was sleeping over so that in the morning he could go look for his father.

He drank his water, then put the glass down. Another voice, one he did not recognize, joined that of William Wilkins. The second voice was deeper and strangely musical.

Jake stood on his tiptoes and leaned toward the window.

"Does it have to be her?" William said.

"You know it does," said the other voice.

"She's only eleven."

"I know," said the voice. "It's early, but he is moving already."

Jake climbed on the kitchen counter to get a better look. He could see a deck just outside. William stood at its edge, leaning on a wooden railing. Beyond the deck, to the right, rose a cherry tree. A strange, tall figure stood under the shadows of its leaves.

"I was hoping it wouldn't happen," William said.

"I was hoping to be long dead by the time he returned."

"I understand."

"I want you to leave her alone. Don't get her involved in this. Don't go near her."

The shadow shifted. "I stopped her once, I told you. She came to the woods last week. I frightened her away. But she has been called by the music. If she comes again, I must help her."

"Then I'll make sure she doesn't come," William said.

"I think you will find there is nothing you can do about it, William," said the shadow. "Just like before."

The shadow shifted. The leaves of the cherry tree shook. Then the figure was not there anymore.

Jake climbed down from the counter as quietly as he could. He went back to the couch, lied down, and pretended to sleep. He remained awake for a long time, unable to forget the shape of the shadow under the tree. The shadow had resembled the silhouette of a tall man with horns protruding from his head.

CHAPTER FOUR

The Forbidden Forest

Sunday morning arrived and Emma rose early.

Jake, still sound asleep when she entered the living room, sprawled on the couch with his arms jutting out from under his blanket at odd angles. She shook the boy awake.

He opened his eyes and blinked in the sunlight.

"Hey, Emma," he said groggily. He sat up and rubbed at his eyes. "Am I at your house?"

"Yeah, come on," she said. "We have to leave before my dad wakes up."

The boy nodded. He stood up, still wearing his clothing from the day before. They slipped out the front door.

Belle Street was a small, quiet street. At that time of morning, it was deserted. They did not bother using the sidewalk. Instead, they made their way toward Lockhart Road right down the middle of the street.

A blue jay watched them walk by from a branch overlooking the road.

"Emma," Jake said. "I saw your dad talking to someone last night. I think they were talking about you."

Emma frowned. "Someone came over last night?"

"No. They were talking outside. I got up to get a drink, and he was talking to someone. They were talking about how you shouldn't go to the forest, but if you did, someone would help you. Something like that."

"They were talking about me?"

"I think so," Jake said. "They were talking about a girl and they said she was eleven. So it has to be you, right?"

"I guess so. But who was he talking to?"

Jake shook his head and looked at the ground.

Emma caught a fluttering of wings in the periphery of her vision. She turned her head to see the blue jay from before fly by and perch itself on a branch farther down the road. The bird turned its head toward them. Emma felt as though it was looking straight at her.

Jake looked up from his shoes. "Emma, it was dark, and I was half asleep. Maybe I dreamed it. He was really tall. I thought he had horns, but maybe it was a hat."

Emma turned her gaze away from the blue jay, forgetting all about it. She froze in place. She opened her mouth, but nothing came out.

"Emma?"

Emma, somewhat regaining her composure, clapped once. "I knew it!" she said. "I knew it wasn't a stupid deer! So my dad knows him? Why hasn't he told me? He said it was my imagination!"

"Hey, don't tell your dad about it, okay?" Jake said. "I don't want him to think I was eavesdropping."

"You were eavesdropping," she said.

"Well, yeah, but I don't want him to think it."

"You really want me to keep this a secret? Do you know how hard that will be?"

"Emma, please," Jake said. "I wasn't supposed to be listening. You're not supposed to go in the forest in the first place, but what if he finds out I told you about this? He will ban you even more. Maybe you'll be grounded forever, and then you won't be able to help me. Maybe he won't let you be friends with me."

Emma did not like the sound of that.

"Besides," Jake said, "it could have been a dream. I have nightmares all the time."

A deer and a nightmare, she thought, were more likely than a man with horns. At least that is what her father would say. She felt some trepidation at the thought of going into the forest if there was a horned creature somewhere inside of it. But then again, if her father was friends with him, then maybe the creature would be friends with her too.

Maybe it had been a deer, and maybe Jake had

had a nightmare, but there was a thought that had been nagging at her since her encounter the other night. What she had seen that night had been horns, like those of a goat, not antlers. As far as she knew, there were no giant goats in Glenridge Forest.

They walked on and arrived at Lockhart Road. Across the street, the forest awaited them. Sunbeams from the east brushed the crowns of the trees with a welcoming, golden gleam. The forest was green except for the odd maple here and there, whose leaves had already started to turn.

Emma led Jake to the spot where she had entered the woods the night she had heard the music. She took a deep breath and stepped forward.

"I'm officially breaking the rules now," she said.

A squirrel scurried in front of them. It reared on its hind paws and stared at Emma.

"What's going on today?" she said. The squirrel scurried away and disappeared into the woods.

"What do you mean?" Jake said.

"That squirrel was staring at me. There was a bird doing it back there too."

Jake rolled his eyes. "Which way do we go?" he said.

"I was just trying to get to the path to the university that night. If we go this way," she said, pointing, "we should run straight into it. The music sounded like it was a little to the right."

"So we go straight and to the right."

Emma nodded. "Straight and then a little to the

right."

She took the lead, trying to retrace her steps from the other night. As they went, she hoped she would hear the music again so they would know exactly which way to go. Otherwise, her plan was for them to move north until they reached the trail that led to the university, then turn to face slightly east and continue walking.

Straight and then a little to the right.

Half an hour later, Emma saw movement through the trees.

"Hey! What are you kids doing here?"

A man in uniform rushed toward them. An imposing dog trotted up ahead of him and reached the children first. The German shepherd sat and stared at Emma.

"What are you doing in the forest?" the man demanded. "Don't you know it's dangerous? Where are your parents?" He wore black pants and a tucked-in grey shirt with the word "SECURITY" stitched in gold thread on a black patch. Beneath the patch hung a laminated identification card with his picture on it next to the name "Aaron Humphries."

"We're just playing, sir," Emma said. She peeked behind him. Beyond the trees she saw a bulldozer and the beginnings of a construction site. "But I think we got lost."

"Do your parents know you're here?"

"No, sir," Emma said.

"You kids better come with me."

Aaron Humphries turned around and headed back in the direction he had come.

Jake glanced at Emma. She shrugged. "I guess we better follow," she said.

The security guard barely glanced back at the children as he led them through the construction site. The German shepherd cantered along beside Emma, staring up at her every so often. House skeletons looked down on them from either side. Most of the structures consisted of bare frames in the shapes of houses, but some were at later stages of construction. There were piles of materials, plywood and light framing, scattered about the place, waiting their turn to become part of a dwelling.

Aaron took them to a little house. It was nothing more than a small box with a door and a window. Emma recognized the structure as a portable building that could be lifted, placed on a truck, and rolled away. A sign next to the door read "Security."

They entered the little house. The German Shepherd sat just inside the door, never taking his eyes off Emma.

Crammed inside the room was a desk, a filing cabinet, and three chairs. The security guard sat them down. He reached into a drawer and brought out a pack of gum. He took a piece, put it in his mouth, and began chewing loudly.

"I'm going to have to call your parents," he said. "What are your names?"

"Emma Wilkins and Jake Milligan," Emma said immediately.

"Milligan? Are you related to Andrew Milligan? The insulator who disappeared?"

Jake nodded. "Yes, sir," he said. "He's my dad."

"I'm sorry," Aaron said. "But why were you kids wandering around here?"

"We're looking for Jake's dad," Emma said. "We were trying to go north and then a little to the right, but I guess we got lost. My dad has forbidden me from coming to the forest so, if he finds out, he will kill me."

Aaron Humphries blinked. "Straight out with it, eh? Well, it's good you're so honest."

The security guard sighed and sat down at his desk. He leaned back in his chair and looked up at the ceiling, his mouth working furiously on the piece of gum.

"All right, listen," he said. "I won't call your parents. But you have to stay out of that forest. The police are doing everything they can to find the missing people. Trust them."

"It's been almost a month," Jake said.

Aaron nodded. "I'm very sorry, kid. But, believe me, everything will be all right."

He stood and led them back outside. They followed him to the construction site's main entrance, passing a large sign propped up on thick, wooden beams. The sign read "Glenridge Glades by Paigely Builders."

"Now go straight home and don't go back in the

forest again," Aaron said. "Stay out of trouble."

"Yes, sir," Emma said.

They started on their way down the road.

"How did we end up there?" Jake said.

"I have no idea. It wasn't on purpose. We were supposed to be heading north. The construction site is east, I think."

They walked on in silence. When they turned down Belle Street, Emma saw a blue jay perched on a branch.

"So what do we do now?" Jake said.

"You still want to do this?"

He nodded.

Emma sighed. She had already broken the rules, anyway. "Okay," she said. "I have a plan."

The blue jay jeered and flew away.

The following day, after school, Jake rode the bus home with Emma and Will. The bus stopped at the corner of Lockhart Road and Belle Street. As soon as it pulled away, Emma grabbed Will by the arm.

"I have to tell you," she said.

"What is it now, Emma?"

"We're going to the forest," she said. "To look for Jake's dad."

"You're crazy," Will said. "Dad will kill you."

She nodded. "Yeah, I know. That's why I need you to promise me you won't snitch. I'll be back before he comes home from work."

Will shook his head. "Emma," he said. "He will

find out. He will kill you."

"I know!" Emma said. "That's why we have to find him quick. If Dad was missing, wouldn't you want me to find him?"

"Only so he could kill you."

"Will!" she whined. "Please, just don't say anything. Just think about if our dad was missing. That's what it's like for Jake. Don't you feel bad at all?"

Will looked at Jake for what seemed like the first time. He looked at the boy's shoes and his worn, ill-fitting clothing. Jake remained silent, but there was a quiet pleading in his eyes.

"Okay," Will said.

"You won't tell?"

"No," he said. "I'm coming with you. Someone has to take care of you."

Emma jumped at him and hugged him. Will indulged her for a moment before disentangling her from his body.

"We better get moving if we are going to do this," he said. "There isn't very much time."

"You're right," Emma said.

They crossed the street and headed straight into the forest.

"We keep the sun to our left," Emma said, as they entered the shade of the trees. "It will keep us going north."

"Why do we want to go north?" Will said.

"There is a singing tree," Emma said, "or a physicist, to the north and a little to the east. Jake's dad heard it the night he disappeared. If we find the tree, or the physicist, we can find Jake's dad, maybe."

"I'm sorry, what?" Will said. "We're looking for a singing tree or a physicist? And we're supposed to find them in the hour and a half before Dad gets home?"

"No," Emma said. "We're going to do this every day."

"That's the plan then? Come to the forest every single day straight from the bus, try to find a singing tree, or a physicist, and then try to get back home before Dad gets there and kills you?"

"Yup."

"Okay," Will said. He turned to Jake. "She's crazy, you know?"

Jake nodded.

"And what's the deal with the physicist?"

"I have no idea," Jake said.

They walked north. Emma made sure they did not deviate from their intended direction. Will kept track of the time with his watch. Jake scanned the surroundings for any clues.

Eventually they arrived, once again, at Glenridge Glades by Paigely Builders.

"Look," Emma said. "It's the construction site."

"How is that possible?" Jake said.

"I don't know. There is no way we could have ended up here."

"Maybe you were distracted," Will said.

"I wasn't!" Emma said. "I kept the sun to our left

the entire time! I mean, mostly. The trees covered it up for a bit, but that's not my fault."

"Well," Will said, glancing at his watch. "We have to go back, anyway. Time's up. We'll just have to pay better attention tomorrow."

They repeated their search the next day, but this time Emma brought a trinket she kept inside the lunch box under her bed. It was a clunky, metal compass with a black and yellow lanyard threaded through a loop on its side.

"I got this thing," Emma said, once inside the forest. "We won't get lost with it. We just have to follow the needle."

They followed the needle until they arrived at a mountainous log that barred their path. Will and Jake climbed on top of it. Emma followed their lead and climbed up as well, though with more difficulty because of her size.

She took advantage of her improved elevation to get a better look at her surroundings. A few feet ahead, a small rabbit sat up on its haunches. It sniffed the air for a moment, then stared straight at Emma. She frowned at it. The rabbit cocked its head to the side before it ran off behind an odd tree. Emma could not tell what kind of tree it was, but its bark looked like peeling scales. The scales formed concentric circles in places.

"Hey, I have an idea," she said.

"What?" Jake said.

"Well," Emma said. "What if we mark the places where we've been? Then we'll know we've already searched there."

Will jumped off the log. "Let's bring a knife and carve arrows into the trees next time," he said.

"No," Emma said. "Don't hurt the trees. I have a better idea."

They continued to search and, as they went, Emma watched the compass more and more often. Something was wrong. They should have arrived at the path already.

Only a minute later, she stopped in her tracks. "Oh no," she said.

A soccer field spread out before them past the trees. Beyond the field rose a familiar building. It was the Harrison Walker Complex, a part of the University of Saint Martin.

"What's the matter?" Jake said.

"We can't be here if we've been going north this entire time," Will said. "There is just more woods to the north and, eventually, a lake. To get to the school you have turn west at some point."

"Huh," Jake said. "That's weird."

"Really weird," Emma said.

"Impossible," Will said. "We're doing something wrong, or maybe your compass is broken."

"I don't think it's broken," she said. "We must be doing something wrong."

"So what are we going to do?" Jake said.

"We're going to get organized," Emma said.

On Wednesday, Emma took a break from searching

the forest. Instead, she trekked up The Hill to the University of Saint Martin. Her destination was the building housing the geography department.

During that time of day, there was plenty of commotion in the hallways. She was the target of more than a few stares, being only eleven and small for her age on top of it.

On the second floor of the building, there was a doorway flanked by rows of great windows. Above the door, silver letters spelt out "Map Library."

Emma peeked inside. A dozen students sat around two large tables in the study area with maps sprawled out in front of them. A few more students dawdled between rows of shelves and cabinets. Behind a desk next to the door, an elderly woman sat typing on a keyboard and peering at a screen.

Emma walked in. She smiled and waved. The woman cocked an eyebrow in response and immediately went back to her typing.

Emma had been to the Map Library before. Her father had brought her here and showed her how to find the maps that were interesting. The maps she liked the most were the old ones with inaccuracies. Today, she was looking for an accurate map.

A shelf in the middle of the room held the local maps. She pulled a large binder out, took it to a nearby table, and spread it open. Inside the binder were a number maps of the area surrounding the university. She turned the pages carefully until she found one made up of stitched-together aerial photographs. The photographs showed the entirety of Glenridge Forest. She took the pages out of the binder and made her way to a photocopier at the back of the room. She made her copies, then carefully put everything back the way she had found it.

On her way out of the Map Library, the woman behind the front desk cocked her eyebrow at her again. Emma waved and smiled.

The hallway was not as crowded as it had been before. She looked both ways, then turned left and made her way toward the exit.

"Hey, Emma!" someone shouted from down the hall. It was Lucy Leroux, the girl from the bus stop and the mall. The girl who had told on her.

"Hello, snitch," Emma muttered under her breath.

Lucy trotted the remaining distance between them.

"Sorry? What?" she said.

"You told on me."

"What do you mean I told on you?"

"You told my dad I was at the mall. I got in trouble."

"I didn't realize you'd get in trouble. I'm sorry. I thought he knew."

Emma studied Lucy's face and decided she was telling the truth. Reluctantly, she conceded that Lucy had had no way of knowing that the expedition to the mall had been a covert operation.

"What do you have there?" Lucy said.

"A map," Emma said.

"Oh? A map of what?"

"The forest. We're looking for someone."

Lucy asked to see the map. Emma handed the pages to her.

"Are these photocopies? Where did you get these?"

Emma pointed back to the Map Library. "From there," she said. "Didn't you know about it?"

Lucy shook her head. "I'm in biology," she said. "Who are you looking for? Why do you need a map?"

She took the pages back. "My friend's dad is missing. He disappeared in the forest. We're searching for him. I'm going to plan it all out."

"Is that safe?"

"Oh, for sure," Emma said, nodding.

"What's your plan?"

Emma took the pages over to a bench nearby and spread them out. She pointed out Glenridge Glades by Paigely Builders. She then slid her finger across to where they normally entered the forest.

"We want to keep track of places we've searched already," Emma said. "So we're going to mark the trees, but I'll also be marking the map."

"You're so smart," Lucy said. "But isn't it going to be hard to use the map from the ground? This is from way up."

"Yeah," Emma said. "That's a big problem, but you can use landmarks." She pointed out a clearing here, an unusually tall tree there. "If you can find these things on the ground, then you know where you are on the map."

"You've thought of a lot, Emma."

"My dad taught me a lot about maps."

"Your dad!" Lucy said. "I was actually on my way to see him!"

"You better go," Emma said. "He hates it when students are late. He complains about it all the time."

Lucy turned to leave. "See you later, Emma," she said.

"See you later, snitch," Emma muttered under her breath.

She spent the rest of the afternoon in her bedroom cutting ribbons out of some old dresses. She came out for dinner and to do homework, but the rest of the time she spent in her room cutting away carefully with a pair of old scissors. The ribbons were approximately the length of her forearm and the width of her index and middle fingers put together.

When the ribbons were ready, she placed them inside a shopping bag.

In math class the next day, Ms Robins' lesson was about measuring and calculating the areas of parallelograms. Emma was still far ahead of the class, and she had figured out all about the subject on her own. So when the lesson was over, and the came time to solve problems in their workbooks, Emma had nothing to do. She could work further ahead but decided instead to refine the search system she had come up with.

She reached into her bag and brought out the aerial photographs of Glenridge Forest. The pages were now taped together neatly into one continuous map. She took a purple marker and set about marking the features of the area that stood out and would be easy to find from the ground.

"Emma!" Ms Robins said. "What is all this?"

"It's a map, Ms Robins."

"I can see that, Emma, but why aren't you working on your math?"

"I finished it already," she said. She took her workbook from her desk and handed it to the teacher. Ms Robins narrowed her eyes, but checked it over anyway.

"I guess you did finish it," she said. "Well, I can't have you playing games in class even if you've done your work. Please put it away. You can work ahead in the book."

"But it's not a game," Emma said.

"No buts, Emma. Put it away now."

Ms Robins glanced at the Strike Board. Emma decided she had better play it safe. She put the map away and took her workbook back from Ms Robins.

By the time class was over, Emma had started to worry that she would run out of work to do very soon.

Over the next few days, ribbons began appearing on the trees of Glenridge Forest. They spread out from the point closest to the intersection of Belle Street and Lockhart Road and fanned out in a northerly direction. There were blue ribbons and red ribbons, and they were tied into neat bows onto the lowest branches. Just as this was happening, as though in response, the leaves of the trees began to change colour.

By marking the forest with ribbons, and marking their progress on her map, Emma could keep track of where they had already searched.

It worked well in the beginning, Emma found, but as they moved farther north, mysterious cracks appeared in the system. Sometimes a mark on the map did not match a ribbon on a tree. It was as though someone was rearranging the ribbons when they were not looking. Will questioned Emma's ability to keep track of the endeavour, but she checked and double-checked her map every night. She let Will take charge of it for a few days, and they found that the same inconsistencies continued to creep up.

At one point, Jake objected that maybe their map was out of date. Emma was forced to admit that it could be a possibility. She made another trip to the university's Map Library and found the original photographs again. The date on the back showed they had been taken only in the previous year.

In two weeks, they ran out of ribbons, and Emma had to find additional clothing from which to cut more. She went down to the basement where the storage boxes were kept. They were strewn about and covered in dust. She found something that she could use in the box farthest back. There were dresses and skirts in it, but they were much too big for Emma. They helped her replenish her ribbon supply.

Emma made sure she was always the one to tie the ribbons. The boys were too careless and could never tie a nice bow. She thought of the ribbons as gifts for the trees.

Despite all her care, the troubling paradoxes continued to arise, and she became increasingly frustrated with their difficulties. She considered asking her father for advice, but could not think of a roundabout way of doing it that would not reveal the entire enterprise to him.

It was at the peak of Emma's frustration when everything came unravelled.

CHAPTER FIVE

Strike Three

I t was Tuesday morning. The sky was angry.

Emma woke up in a grey mood. She could feel, with no need to look, that it was cloudy outside. With heavy feet, she slid out of bed and prepared for the day ahead.

Emma stood close to Briardale Middle School's main entrance.

Jake's bus arrived. The children inside filed out. Most of them wore hooded sweatshirts or light jackets. The modest swarm marched past her and into the school. There was no sign of Jake.

She hesitated, not sure about what to do. There was probably a reasonable explanation why Jake was not there but, in the back of Emma's mind, something of a small panic began to grow. It was the fear that Jake had disappeared. That he had hidden from her again.

When she finally went to her classroom, Ms Robins glared at her. The teacher took a pointed glance at her watch. Emma lowered her head and made her way to her desk.

The day's math lesson was about reflections, rotations, and translations of shapes. Emma knew all about the subject already, having worked far head, but she tried her best to pay close attention and not think about the empty chair near the door.

When it was time for recess, Emma stopped by the teacher's desk and asked her about Jake. If there was a reason for his absence, then his mother might have called the school. Ms Robins told her she had heard nothing about the boy.

Emma went outside. The sky was black. She sat in her usual spot on the swing, one arm wrapped around its steel chain, and hugged herself against the wind. She had not brought a jacket. She twirled her feet in the air in small, timid circles and glanced around at the drab morning. The chill wind had swept away all the joy from the playground. The children drifted without aim, like wandering ghosts lost in a graveyard. She wanted to race home, or to the university, and find her father.

At lunchtime, Emma found herself alone on the rock at Wizard Falls. She had hoped Jake would be there waiting there for her as she came up over the hill, that he had slept late and missed the bus in the morning. But their secret hiding place had been empty.

Emma's lunch sat untouched beside her. She had the strange feeling that she was waiting for something but did not know what.

The wind picked up and howled through the trees. She wrapped her arms around herself and watched the trees sway with the wind before rolling black clouds, for a moment fascinated with the sight.

The sudden boom of thunder made her jump. A moment or two after her heart settled down, the first few drops of cold rain sputtered into the creek nearby. She looked up to the sky. A giant raindrop landed on her cheek. The drop was followed by a downpour.

Emma gathered her lunch and jumped off the rock. She ran up the hill. Upon reaching the crest, she slowed down to negotiate the steep descent on the other side. She clambered down the slippery slope carefully but could not hold on to her lunch bag. She watched it slide and tumble into the shallow water below.

Slowly, she picked her way down.

The bank of the creek had already turned to mud. She took a tentative step forward. Her foot sank into the sludge. Mud covered her shoes and her jeans, up to the knees, by the time she crossed the old log and stepped onto the far bank.

Emma slumped all the way back to school without rushing, dejected, and figuring that she was already as miserable as she could be. She entered the school through one of the side entrances, staring down at her muddy shoes. Dirty water dripped off her clothes and onto the floor.

"Emma Wilkins."

She stopped in her muddy tracks and looked up. It was Mr Clarence, the school principal.

"Hello, Mr Clarence," she said.

"You're all wet, Emma. Whatever were you doing outside?"

"I don't know, Mr Clarence," she said.

The principal raised his eyebrows. "Come with me, young lady," he said.

"Yes, Mr Clarence."

She followed him down the hall to the administrative section of the school.

"You're in real trouble now, Emma," she whispered.

"Did you say something?"

"No, sir."

Inside his office, he told Emma to wait a moment, then left the room. The principal returned with a heavy towel and handed it to her. He sat down behind his desk. Emma did her best to dry off.

"Sit down," Mr Clarence said when she had finished.

She folded the towel, placed it on a chair in front of his desk, and then sat on it.

"How are things, Emma?"

"Fine."

"So you don't know why you were outside?"

"No, sir."

He tapped his pen on his desk. Emma could not help but fidget while she waited to hear exactly how much trouble she was in.

"You've been playing with Jake Milligan, haven't you? Do you know about his recent misfortunes?"

Emma looked up. "Yes, sir," she said. "I know his dad went missing. Do you know where he is today, Mr Clarence? Jake, I mean."

He took a clipboard from the corner of his desk and flipped over a few pages. "Milligan, Jake," he said. "Absent. No reason given. Hopefully, he will bring a note tomorrow."

Emma nodded.

"Well, Emma," Mr Clarence said. "The reason I brought you in here, aside from the fact that you were soaked, and your shoes are covered in mud, is that I wanted to let you know that if something is wrong, anything, my door is open to you."

"Sir?"

"You're a good student. I looked at your records. But this year hasn't got off to a great start, has it?"

"No, sir."

"Your grades are excellent, but your behaviour has been upsetting Ms Robins."

"Yes, sir."

"Don't be afraid to come to me if you need help with anything at all. That goes for Jake as well."

"Yes, sir."

He took a blank piece of paper and scribbled on it. "Here," he said. "Take this to Ms Robins so you won't get in trouble."

"Thank you, sir," she said.

Emma stood up and left the principal's office. She tracked mud all the way down the hall and up the stairs to the second floor.

She reached her classroom and peeked around the doorway. Ms Robins stood at the chalkboard, scratching the chalk against its surface in abrupt, forceful strokes.

Emma took a deep breath and stepped into the room. Ms Robins turned from the board. Before the teacher could speak, Emma rushed to her, waving the life-saving note above her head. Ms Robins snatched the note from her and scanned it over with darting eyes. She frowned, crumpled the paper up, and threw it at the trash can next to her desk. She missed.

Jeff Johns laughed. A furious glance from the teacher turned his laughter into a sudden gargle.

Ms Robins turned back to Emma. The teacher pointed toward Emma's desk without saying a word.

Emma slouched to her chair and sat down. Her clothes were still damp. She shivered. Her teeth chattered.

Ms Robins watched her for a moment. She then turned back to the chalkboard and resumed her lesson. Emma tried her best to appear fascinated.

The afternoon wore on, and the rain continued to beat upon the row of windows at the side of the classroom. The students were allowed to stay inside during recess. Emma was glad.

She spread out her map of Glenridge Forest on her desk, glancing for a moment at the empty chair where Jake should have been. He was probably sick at home, and she had worried about him all day for no reason. She would have to help him catch up with what he had missed today, starting with the lesson on translations of geometric shapes.

Perhaps, she thought, she could apply her map to the lesson to make it more interesting. Trees were just lots of different shapes put together, after all.

An idea occurred to her. She imagined a circle drawn near the corner of a page of graph paper. If she translated it to the centre of the page, the circle would remain exactly the same, only its location would change. But what if it was not a circle, but a tree? What if it was not her ribbons that were being moved around? What if it was the trees themselves being translated?

If Andrew Milligan had gotten lost in the forest, all he would have needed to do was to walk in a single direction and, eventually, he would have come out of it. But if the trees could move around and change the layout of the forest, then maybe he was trapped inside a sort of labyrinth.

But Emma realized that the trees moving around would not be enough to explain why she and the boys had never been able to stay on a course due north, even with the help of a compass. There had to be more to it. Perhaps the compass really was broken, or something was interfering with it. Perhaps it was not just the trees shifting around, but the entire forest.

She took a hard look at her map and decided she would go back to the university to make more copies. They would use a different copy each time they went into the forest. If the trees were moving, there could be some pattern to their translation. If they kept track of how the forest changed each day, they might figure out the pattern.

"So cool!" she said, more loudly than intended.

She looked up. The classroom was silent. The students were all at their desks, heads turned in her direction. Suzie Collins was rolling her eyes.

Recess had ended. She had not noticed.

"Emma!" Ms Robins said from the front of the room. She stormed to Emma's desk. "This again? I told you, you can't be playing around during my class. You've been a nuisance since day one, Emma Wilkins. Just because your father is a university professor doesn't mean you can do whatever you want!"

"Ms Robins, I…"

"I nothing! I've had just about enough of you!"

The teacher charged to the front of the room and picked up a permanent marker from her desk. Beside Emma's name on the Strike Board, she wrote a third "X," much bigger, and sloppier, than the previous two.

"Strike three, Emma Wilkins. To the principal's office. Now!"

And so Emma found herself back at Mr Clarence's

office.

The principal raised an eyebrow when he saw her standing at the door. He motioned for her to come in. The towel she had used earlier was still draped across the chair. She made her way back to it and sat down.

"What's the matter, Emma?"

"Ms Robins sent me, sir," she said.

"Now, why did she do that?"

"I disrupted the class. She gave me my third strike."

"Are you playing baseball in there?"

"No, sir, it's just that there is this board…"

"I know, Emma," he said. "It was just my little joke. Well, here's the thing. Ms Robins takes her strikes very seriously so I can't just send you back there. She will kill me, figuratively, I think, if I don't give you detention for at least one day."

"Okay, Mr Clarence," Emma said.

"Not today, though. I think today you've been through enough. Maybe tomorrow at lunchtime. Just come to my office then."

Emma nodded and stood up, wondering if the principal was so nice to everyone. Before she made it to the door, he spoke again.

"Emma, you know we have to call your family?"

"Yes, sir. My dad."

"Maybe I can tell the secretary to hold off until tomorrow so you can explain this to your parents yourself first."

"No parents, Mr Clarence. Only a dad. But yes,

please. Thank you, sir, Mr Clarence."

As soon as school let out for the day, Rebecca Robins made her way to the main office of Briardale Middle School. There was no one there except for the secretary, who sat behind a counter typing into her keyboard.

"Hey, Dory," Rebecca said.

"Hello, Rebecca," Dory said, looking up.

Rebecca leaned against the counter. "Listen, did you call Emma Wilkins' parents yet?"

Dorothy stopped typing. "No, I didn't," she said. "George said to wait until tomorrow."

Rebecca frowned. "Now, why would that be?"

"I have no idea. He didn't say."

"Can I have their number?" Rebecca said. "I think I need to talk to her parents myself. It's important."

It was still raining when Emma's bus arrived at her stop.

Will and Emma ran all the way home. They went to their respective bedrooms without saying a word. Emma was grateful. Will was good at recognizing when she was not in the mood for talking.

She changed into her pyjamas and a pair of slippers. She wanted the day to end, but she knew the hardest part was yet to come. She had to tell her father what she had done, and the trouble she had gotten into.

With a sigh, she reached underneath her bed and brought out the yellow lunch box. From it, she withdrew the old, tattered copy of her favourite book. She climbed onto her bed and snuggled into her blankets.

Emma opened the book carefully. It took her, in her mind, to a hole in the ground, where she found a measure of quiet comfort before tired eyelids closed on their own and she fell asleep.

When Emma woke up, it was dark outside. Her book rested on her chest against her chin. She blinked a few times in confusion. It took her a moment to recognize the voices. One of them belonged to her father. The other voice was also familiar. She climbed out of bed and put her book under her pillow.

She crept to the living room. Her father was speaking, but he cut himself short as she entered. Seated across from him was Lucy Leroux.

Lucy looked up. Her eyes were streaked with tears.

William Wilkins beckoned Emma over. She sat on the edge of the armchair opposite the window. The three of them formed a neat triangle.

"Emma…" William said. He shook his head. A pulse of panic beat in Emma's chest when she saw his expression. A deep-set frown dominated his features. He took off his glasses, closed his eyes, and rubbed the bridge of his nose. Emma had seldom seen him this way.

"You're such a good girl, Emma, but lately…"

"Dad," Emma said, "what is happening?"

"It's my fault," he said. "I've just let you run off and do whatever you want. Your mother—"

Lucy Leroux spoke up in a small voice. "Professor, maybe I should go?"

"No, no, it's all right. I'm sorry, Lucy." He turned to Emma and sighed. "I know you've been in the forest," he said. "That's why Lucy is here."

Emma stood up. She was in a great deal of trouble, more than she had thought.

The rest of the day's events came back to her. Jake was missing. She had her third strike at school. Now, on top of it all, she had to explain her excursions into the forest.

Then there was Lucy.

"You did it to me again," she said, more harshly than intended. But once the words were out, she could not stop herself. "You're just a giant snitch!"

Lucy looked down at the floor.

"Emma!" William said. He stood up. "Why are you being so difficult lately? First this obsession with the forest, and now I get a call at work that you have detention. What is wrong with you?"

The words pierced her chest.

Her thoughts were jumbled. Lucy had betrayed her again. Mr Clarence had also broken his promise. Jake was lost. Her father was yelling at her, and she could not remember ever seeing him so angry. He seemed like a different person.

"I'm sorry," she said, and tears began to flow.

William opened his mouth, but Emma did not hear the words that came out. At that moment, a cascade of sound inundated the room.

It was music. Emma heard the same instrument she had heard in the forest, but this time many others had joined it. It was a symphony, sad and longing.

She searched for the source of the sound, glancing frantically out the window and all around the room. Lucy and her father remained as before, as though unaware of the deluge.

"Don't you hear that?" Emma shouted. She could not hear her own voice. The music filled her. It was all she could hear. She brought her hands up to her ears. The music did not stop. She dropped to her knees.

She took a glance to the side and saw Will standing in the hallway. His lips moved silently.

Emma closed her eyes. "I'm sorry, I'm sorry," she said, sobbing, and it was all she could do.

When she opened her eyes again, she saw her father take a step toward her. His face was a strange mask of anger and confusion. For a moment, she could not recognize the man behind the mask. It was as though a stranger had taken her father's place. Fear engulfed her. The music overwhelmed her. She ran.

Out the door and into the night, Emma ran.

CHAPTER SIX

A Girl and a Tree

Emma ran.

Pink slippers slapped the cold, wet street as she ran. The rain had subsided to a light drizzle. The street lamps shone feebly, their frail light forming ghostly islands in the dark. She did not know where she was going, only that she was running away.

Water sprayed up all the way to her face when she stepped in a pothole. She barely slowed down, leaving a slipper behind. Several lopsided steps later, she kicked the other slipper away. Coarse asphalt pricked at her feet but did not slow her down.

Emma ran. She did not see the darkness of Glenridge Forest rise before her until she was almost inside it.

She skidded to a halt on the grassy shoulder beside the road. The forest loomed up in front of her.

She hunched down and gasped for breath. Her feet hurt. The music roared inside her head.

She tried to calm down and think things through. This was what they had been looking for all this time: the music in the forest. Her mission was to find its source. But this music was so loud that it seemed to be everywhere at once. It was not the quiet instrument she had heard before, but a torrent of sound too overwhelming to follow. Nevertheless, if the music was in the forest, that was where she needed to go.

She took a deep breath and stepped under the cover of the trees. Darkness and silence immediately enveloped her. The frail tendrils of light from the street lamps disappeared. The music ceased.

Alone in the dark, in the quiet that followed, Emma was afraid. She stood in place for a long time, not knowing what to do.

Something howled in the distance. The noises of the night drifted to her gradually. They were soon joined by a different sound altogether. It was the deep groan of straining wood. The image of walking trees came to her unbidden.

Her eyes adjusted to the darkness slowly. First, she became aware of a multitude of bright eyes that stared toward her from all over. They were small, round eyes that, she presumed, belonged to little critters. Then the forest took shape. Darkness resolved into the dark, familiar profiles of tree trunks and shrubs. There was no trace of Lockhart Road. As far as she could tell, the forest surrounded her.

Emma could not tell which way she had come from. Disoriented, lost and afraid, she whispered into the night.

"Help me," she said.

The music returned, but it was not the overwhelming roar from before. It was quiet, sweet, and comforting. It was a single instrument, like a violin. The sound drifted to her from somewhere deep in the forest.

"Thank you," Emma said. She moved toward the sound, picking her way carefully through the forest woods. She heard the scurrying of little feet. The eyes that watched her moved about between the trees and followed her. She heard the flapping of wings and looked up. Gleaming eyes stalked her from above. The woods groaned.

Emma walked on through the forest, followed all the while by her mysterious retinue.

When the tree appeared, it happened quickly and suddenly. One moment, there was only forest before her. Then the next, the trees in front and the clouds above both parted. The trees revealed a clearing. The clouds let the moon illuminate it. It was as though a great curtain had been pulled back.

In the centre of the clearing stood a great oak, old and gnarled. Brown-green leaves crowned its vast trunk, the uppermost layer shimmering in the moonlight.

Emma stepped into the clearing. Her procession

did not follow. The multitude of shining eyes remained behind under the cover of the trees, though they watched her still, blinking now and then. The woods ceased their groaning.

Emma approached the tree slowly, certain that it was the source of the music.

"Are you singing?" she said timidly.

She reached out and touched its rough bark with her fingertips. There was heat there, an undulating warmth that seemed to respond to her touch. She placed her hand against the tree. The music swelled, and the warmth passed into her like a rolling wave. They were comforting, the warmth and the music.

Emma knelt down. She listened to the music and felt the tree's caress. It put her at ease and made her forget all the bad things that had happened that day. It would not be hard to forget herself, close her eyes, sleep, and dream long dreams while the tree sang its lullaby. She wondered if Andrew Milligan slept somewhere in the forest beside his own tree, simply having lost track of time.

The earth shook and thunder roared.

Emma jumped to her feet. In the darkness surrounding the clearing, there was a flurry of activity as the creatures that had followed her all this way fled back into the forest.

"What is happening?"

The leaves rustled above her. She looked up and saw the branches of the tree flutter in unison. Something dropped to the ground nearby. Emma approached the object. It was a smooth rod, plain and bare except for a line of holes running up its side.

"A flute?" she said.

"Yes."

The answer came from the darkness beyond the clearing. "Take it," said the voice, deep and musical.

Emma picked up the flute and clutched it to her chest. The creature stepped into the clearing under the moonlight. The voice belonged to something resembling a man, tall and lean. Ram-like horns protruded from his head. His upper body was bare. His lower half was covered in fur, ending in cloven hooves in place of feet. A human-like face, unnaturally elongated and seemingly on the verge of grinning, regarded Emma with an unsettling, indecipherable expression.

"Be afraid, Emma," the creature said. "But do not fear me. Fear the one who comes next."

"Who—" Emma said, and it was all she could say before thunder interrupted her. Thunder from inside the forest, closer this time than the last.

"Call me Domino," the creature said. "I'm a faun of the forest. You have little time, for he is almost here. You should not have come at night. I stopped you once before in the rain."

"I don't understand what's happening," Emma said, her voice cracking.

The faun uttered something like a sigh. He nodded to the flute that she held before her.

"Take care of that," he said. "It is a gift from the tree. But now you must go. Return when the sun has risen, and I will explain."

"How do I leave this place?"

"I can remain unseen in the forest whenever I please," the faun said, "but you must rely on other means until you learn how it is done." He motioned toward the great oak. "He will take you where you need to go."

He raised his hand toward Emma. She took it, slowly and apprehensively. The faun moved quickly. Before Emma could react, he snatched her up with ease and threw her toward the tree. She braced herself for impact, but a sliver of light materialized at the place where she would have struck the oak. The sliver widened into a circular portal.

Emma plunged into the light. She saw the faun dart into the forest a mere instant before a great beast burst into the clearing. The newcomer had the head of a great bull, but it stood upright and massive. Its body resembled that of a brutally large man. The creature's eyes burned directly toward Emma.

She tried to cry out in fear, but she was ripped apart into a million pieces by the light of the portal.

Emma found herself sitting on a bench next to a tall woman in medical scrubs. The woman's eyes were opened so wide they almost quivered. The woman stood up in a hurry and rushed into a crowded bus shelter. The people in the shelter were also staring at Emma. When they realized she was looking back at them, they all turned away at once.

Emma could not remember how she had arrived there, or much of anything at all. She was holding a crude wooden flute in her hands. The musical instrument sparked a vague memory about a dark forest and an old tree, but it was only a shadowy image she did not understand.

A black cat wandered over and jumped up on the bench beside her.

"Hello, Mr Cat," Emma said.

The cat regarded her with penetrating eyes. He turned his head toward the people in the bus shelter.

"They see a girl appear out of nowhere and that's how they react," the cat said. "They try to disappear her right back again."

Emma blinked. "I can talk to animals!" she said with delight, raising her arms in the air.

The cat blinked back at her. "I can't understand anything you're saying," he said. "You're just talking nonsense like the rest of them." He leaped from the bench and ran off across a lawn and around an apartment building.

Emma watched the cat go. She lowered her arms and frowned. After a moment, she raised her arms up again.

"I can listen to animals!" she said with delight.

There was some awkward shuffling inside the bus shelter.

A bus pulled up. Several travellers cast wary glances back toward Emma as they boarded.

When the bus drove away, Emma took in her surroundings. It was a cool morning on a busy street. Cars zipped by in both directions on the four-lane road in front of her. Across the street, a sprawling parking lot spread out before a hospital building.

"He'll take me where I need to go," Emma said. Someone had told her that recently. "A hospital? Am I hurt?"

She checked herself over. Her feet were bare. She was dressed in wet, dirty pyjamas. She appeared uninjured except for the soles of her feet. They were nicked and bruised but did not need immediate medical attention aside from a good cleaning and a couple of bandages. But maybe the hospital would have some clean clothes for her to wear.

She made her way to the street corner and pushed the button for the crosswalk.

"Emma!"

A boy waved at her from across the street. He stood next to a short, stout woman with a look of shock and confusion on her face.

The traffic light changed from red to green. The boy ran across the street, leaving the woman behind. She scrambled to catch up.

"Emma, you're filthy," the boy said upon reaching her. "What are you doing here?"

She stared at the boy. He looked vaguely familiar.

She had seen his eyes before. The boy shifted uncomfortably under her study.

"Emma?"

"Hold still!" Emma said. She stood on her tiptoes and narrowed her eyes, leaning slightly forward to look into his. Memories of a sad boy sitting on a rock trickled back into her.

"Jake!" she said.

As though a floodgate had opened, the rest of her memory surged back inside of her. The great oak in the clearing. The faun of the forest. The monster who had emerged from the darkness. She had fallen into a portal of light, and now she was here somehow.

Victoria Milligan arrived behind the boy. She opened her mouth to speak, but no words came out. She shook her head.

"Hello, Mrs Milligan," Emma said.

Victoria brought one hand up to her head. She took a deep breath and seemed to regain her composure.

"Call me Vicky," she said. "What are you doing here? Look at you! What happened?"

Emma took a breath. "There was a singing tree in the forest, and he gave me this flute. Then a thing with horns came, and there was another bigger thing with horns. It was scary, but the smaller one pushed me into the tree, and I showed up here. It was night then, but it's day now. I'm not sure what day it is, though."

"I see," Victoria Milligan said. "Where are your

shoes? Why are you wearing pyjamas? Where is your father, dear?"

"I don't know. At home or at work, maybe? I don't know what time it is. He's probably worried about me. I ran away crying!"

"Oh, I'm sorry to hear that," Victoria said. "I think I understand what happened now, Emma. You sure got very far running away. Did you take a bus here?"

"No, Mrs Vicky," Emma said. "I took a portal."

Victoria nodded slowly. "Of course, Emma," she said. "Well, we need to get you home. And we need to let your father know you're safe." She led them to the same bench Emma had been sitting on before. The children sat down. Victoria took her mobile phone out of her purse.

"Why were you at the hospital?" Emma said to Jake.

"Grandpa," Jake said. "He's sick."

"I'm sorry," Emma said. "I hope he's okay."

"He's a little better, they said."

"That's why you weren't at school? What day is it?"

"We've been here since yesterday, Emma. Today is Wednesday. Is it true that you found the tree? What about my dad?"

"I'm sorry," Emma said, shaking her head.

The bus ride home took almost an hour and a half. During that time, Emma sat next to Jake and recounted the previous night's events.

"But why did the tree send you to the hospital?"

Jake said when she had finished.

"I think it's because you were there," Emma said. "The faun, Domino, said that it would take me where I needed to go."

"But why would it send you to me?"

Emma looked down at her lap and was silent for a moment. She blushed. "I think it's because I was worried I'd lost you," she said.

Jake said nothing. He turned toward the window. The colour rose in his cheeks as well. They rode on in silence for a few moments. The boy was lost in thought.

"Emma," he said, turning back to face her. "I want to talk to the faun. Maybe he knows where my dad went. Maybe he went through a portal too."

"Maybe you're right," she said. "I hadn't thought of that. We'll talk to him, Jake. I promise."

Upon arriving at the Saint Martin Bus Terminal, they transferred to another bus. This was a local bus that took them to the corner of Belle Street and Lockhart Road. Victoria Milligan insisted they ride with Emma and walk her all the way home to see her safe, even though they lived across town from her.

As they reached the door to her house, it swung open before they could ring the doorbell. Emma's father stood just inside. His face was pale. He took off his glasses and rubbed at his eyes.

"Good morning, Mrs Milligan," he said.

"Call me Vicky, please," Victoria said. "Well, here she is, safe and sound."

"Thank you so much for bringing her all this way. I'm sorry for all the trouble. Would you like to come in for a cup of coffee, perhaps?"

"Oh, no, we really should get going. Thank you. It has been a long couple of days, and we should get on home. I'm just glad Emma is back here safe. I'm sure the two of you have some talking to do so we better just leave you to it."

They said their goodbyes. Jake and his mother turned toward the street. Emma and her father stood at the door in silence and watched them go. When the Milligans disappeared down the road, they went inside.

William closed the door.

"Dad, I'm sorry—" Emma began.

"Are you tired? Do you need rest?" he said hurriedly.

"No, not really," she said. "It doesn't feel like a whole night went by."

"It didn't for you. Put on some shoes, Emma. We're going to the forest."

"I don't understand," she said.

"I know. I'll explain on the way."

Emma rushed along beside her father, holding tightly onto the flute she had been given, nearly having to trot to keep up with his swift, long steps. He had said nothing since the moment they had left the house.

They entered the shade of Glenridge Forest. The

air was still cool from the rain of the night before. Three small chickadees sat in a neat row on a low branch nearby. They chirped when they saw her. It sounded to her as though they said, "Emma! Emma! Emma!" in their tinny bird voices.

"He told you to come and that he would find you, correct?"

"Yes, Dad," Emma said. "How do you know?"

"You met Domino," he said. "I know him. That's how I knew you had disappeared somewhere. I came looking for you when you ran away, Emma. Domino stopped me from entering the forest. He promised he would protect you. He said there were dark things about. I've known him for a long time, and I trust him."

He motioned for them to go, and they started walking through the forest. The little birds flew from branch to branch, keeping pace with them.

"He then came to me in the night and told me what happened to you. How you'd been sent away from danger, though he didn't know where."

"How do you know him, Dad?"

"Emma, there's a lot I've kept from you," he said. A faraway look came over him. He gazed into the forest as though searching for something, or someone, but then he only sighed and turned back to her.

"Emma," he said. "You're special. I've tried to protect you from this, to keep you from this world, but it's too late now. You've been recognized."

"I don't understand, Dad."

"I know," he said. "It's complicated. When you came here last night, you were being watched. The forest knows about you now, and there are dark things in the night that would mean you harm. Dark things I can't protect you from."

"Things want to hurt me? Like the monster I saw last night?"

He nodded slowly, a pained expression on his face. "Domino will help. That's the reason I'm bringing you to him. He has been trying to convince me to do so for a very long time. I refused and refused, but now I have no choice. I can't protect you, but he can teach you to defend yourself. He has promised not to involve you in anything more than that."

Emma saw the faun ahead. He was leaning against a tree playing the flute that he carried. It was a cheerful, pleasant melody.

William stopped walking and waved to him. Domino lowered the flute from his lips.

"Go ahead, Emma," her father said. "He will not teach you unless you go alone."

"Alone?" she said. "Dad, I'm scared."

He put a hand on her shoulder for a moment then knelt down and hugged her close. "I'm very sorry, Emma. I knew this day would come. I only wish it hadn't been so soon." He kissed her forehead. "Now, remember, he will only teach you how to defend yourself. That's it. Nothing more."

He stood up and went back the way they had come.

Emma stepped forward. The faun watched her intently as she made her way to him.

"I'm glad you came," he said. "Do you know why you are here?"

"Not really," she said. "I don't understand any of it."

"Emma," the faun said. "We need you to save the world."

CHAPTER SEVEN

The Missing

Aaron Humphries arrived at the security office and bid goodnight to the daytime guard. He pet Oliver, went to the desk, and signed the security log. Aaron did not enjoy working nights. He did not understand why the Paigely Builders construction site needed a security guard there at all times. He figured that it had to do with company policies and bureaucracy.

He opened one of the desk drawers and took out a long, hefty flashlight. He took a piece of gum from his pocket and put it in his mouth.

With a sigh, he went out into the cool evening and began his first round of the night. Oliver strode along by his side. Aaron's usual round took him about the perimeter of the construction site, along the edge of the forest, and down to the main entrance, beside the sign announcing the construction of Glenridge Glades. There, he turned up the gravel road that snaked through the middle of the housing project.

He was somewhere near the centre of the site when he saw a faint light emanating from one of the half-finished houses. He headed toward it. The exterior of the house was all exposed plywood.

He climbed the rough steps in front of the door and went inside. Two men looked up from their work. Aaron nodded to each of them.

"Bill. Joel."

"Hey, Aaron," Bill said. He was the older of the two. Grey hair was beginning to crop up in his otherwise dark hair. He put down a panel of insulation and walked over.

"How are you guys doing?" Aaron said.

Bill shrugged. "Well enough, considering," he said. "Still not used to not having Andrew around. Sometimes I still expect to see him working when I turn a corner."

They walked over to the doorless entrance of the house, their boots thudding on the bare, wooden floor. They looked out into the failing light.

"How's Joel doing?" Aaron said quietly.

"You can imagine," Bill said. "He plays it off like it doesn't bother him as much as it does, but I can tell. He's in bad shape."

"Can't say I blame him. Vanished just like that, didn't he? Heard some music or something?"

Bill grimaced and looked away for a moment. "We were working. He said he heard music from the forest. We laughed it off. When I left with Joel for the night, Andrew was getting in his car, but he must have stayed to check it out."

"He'd just moved here, right?"

"From the big city," Bill said. "With his wife and his kid."

"What are you guys talking about?" Joel said from where he crouched. He stood up and joined them.

"We were just wondering about that Steven Marks," Bill said. "You ever talk to him?"

Joel shook his head.

"Me neither," Bill said. "He was an older guy, wasn't he?"

"Yeah." Joel sat down on the steps and pulled out a pack of cigarettes from his shirt pocket. He fumbled with the pack and took a cigarette out.

"Those things will kill you," Aaron said.

Joel nodded. "I know. I wish I could quit."

"I used to smoke," Aaron continued. "Try chewing gum instead."

A silence followed. Aaron decided he better get back to his rounds. He walked around Joel and descended the steps to where Oliver sat.

The dog stood suddenly. His body stiffened and his ears perked up.

"It's all right, Ollie," Aaron said. "What is it?"

Oliver paid him no mind. The German shepherd glared toward the northwest, where the forest was thickest.

"What's with him?" Joel said from the steps.

"I don't know," Aaron said. "I think he hears

something."

Joel stood up. Bill joined them. They stood in silence, looking to the northwest. Beyond the half-built houses and machinery rose the forest, dark and imposing. A sea of shadow flowed and swirled among the trees. Dark, grey clouds lingered in the sky above the canopy of the woods.

"I don't hear anything," Bill said.

Joel held up his hand. "Hang on," he said. "I think I hear something."

Aaron slowed his breathing, straining to hear. For a moment, there was only silence. Then, from far off in the distance, gentle music drifted to him in the still night air. A vibrant melody, like that of a string instrument, invited him to follow.

"I hear it too," Bill said. He sounded far away. "The music. It's Andrew's music."

Aaron listened. The music in the forest surged like a tidal wave.

"What are we waiting for?" Joel said. He broke away from the group.

Aaron shook his head. Something was wrong.

"Let's go, Aaron," Bill said. He followed his friend and co-worker.

Aaron opened his mouth to argue. No words came out. He could not think. He glanced around helplessly. Oliver was not there anymore.

"Ollie," he said. "Where did that dog go? And when did it get so dark?"

The darkness was thick around him. Night had fallen. He had not noticed. He fingered his flashlight. Maybe Bill and Joel were right. Maybe he needed to find the music then everything would be all right. Yes, the music would make everything all right.

Aaron Humphries turned on his flashlight and strode after the other two men.

They arrived at a clearing. A great monument stood at its centre: A towering tree with branches like long, contorted fingers reaching out toward them.

"Something is wrong," Aaron said. "How did we get here?"

"We walked here from the construction site," Bill said. "I think."

Joel nodded slowly. "Yeah, that's right. I tripped on that branch, remember?"

Aaron searched his memory. He remembered offering his hand to Joel. He remembered a dog and a security office. The rest of his memories were faded images he did not understand.

"I need to report this," he said. "Yes. That's what I should have done in the first place."

The roar of thunder erupted inside the forest. A demon exploded into the clearing.

The beast was tall, eight feet or more. Its head was that of a bull. Its nostrils flared in anger, and its eyes burned with crimson fire. The creature's horns were long and black, tapering to fine points. Its body was an exaggeration of a man, impossibly large and powerful. The monster's chest heaved with each of its breaths.

Aaron tried to scream. Before he could do so, the monster was upon them. It was violently agile.

He fell back and landed hard on the ground. Bill and Joel were snatched up like puppets. The monster's hands were big enough to lift Bill off the ground by his thigh.

Joel hung in the air by his elbow. He kicked at the monster. The demon closed his fist. Joel screamed as his elbow shattered.

Aaron struggled to his feet. The monster made his way to the tree. A line of light appeared there. It grew into a luminous circle. The beast threw the screaming men inside the tree, one by one.

Aaron turned to run. There was a sudden blur in front of him. The demon now stood barring his way. Despair overtook him as he found himself lifted effortlessly into the air. He could feel the raw power of the creature and knew that that there was no point in resisting.

As the monster carried him toward the tree, he saw a young woman enter the clearing. He did not believe she could be real.

The monster threw Aaron Humphries into the portal of light.

Rebecca Robins was running.

She had left her house at precisely eight o'clock as was her routine. It was a stringent one she rarely deviated from. Her weekdays were spent always in the same manner: she remained at work at Briardale Middle School to do marking and lesson planning until five o'clock; she arrived home at five-thirty and made dinner, which she ate at six o'clock at her dinner table; at six-thirty, she went to her living room with a cup of tea and read a novel until exactly seven forty-five, when she changed into her running clothes. Rebecca Robins jogged for an hour every night.

There was a jogging trail that snaked through an old quarry near Rebecca's house. For years, she had run that trail and only that trail. Tonight, she was running along a dimly lit street near the woods, unsure how she had arrived there.

Something had been nagging at the back of her mind all afternoon. She felt as though she had forgotten something important, but she could not remember what it was no matter how hard she tried. It probably had to do with that girl Emma and her awful behaviour. The little girl was a monster, hell-bent on creating chaos in her class. She had given the girl her third strike that afternoon. She had called the girl's father. Hopefully, that would help set her straight.

A cool drop of water fell on the back of her neck. She looked up with the fear that it had started to rain again. Above her head, several branches reached out from the woods and above the sidewalk. Leaves swayed in a light breeze.

Rebecca stopped running. She remembered why

she was here. A sweet music had come to her in the night. It had called her to the forest.

She turned to face the woods. She shook her head. What a ridiculous idea, she thought. Music in the forest. It was like something that little monster Emma would have dreamt up.

She turned to leave and find her way home.

Gentle music flowed into her from the darkness under the trees.

Rebecca did not know how long she followed the music. The forest was still damp from the rain. She hardly noticed. The music was sweet and lovely, and it made her happy.

Even as she came within sight of the glade, she was not taken aback by the violence within. Two men struggled with a monster, while another cowered on the ground.

One man screamed.

The monster dragged the two men to a tree. A circle of light appeared there, and they were thrown into it. The third man barely put up a fight as the great hands of the fiend picked him up. He looked directly at Rebecca.

She raised her hand awkwardly, and then the man disappeared into the light.

Rebecca took delicate steps forward. The monster watched her. There was raw power in its body and fire in its eyes. She felt afraid. The creature tensed up as though readying for an assault. Before

Rebecca could panic, the music swelled and filled her senses again.

She turned toward the tree and, though she could not forget that the monster was there, its presence did not seem to matter as much as it had a moment before.

The school teacher smiled dreamily and took brisk steps toward the tree. The beautiful music was coming from inside of it.

She tried to peer into the light, but her gaze could not penetrate it. A small voice in her head cautioned that this was dangerous. Part of her recoiled at the strangeness of it. But the music was so sweet that it made her heart ache. It called to her and made her want to be close to it. She needed to find its source.

Rebecca Robins took one last look at the world around her and at the creature standing guard near the tree.

She stepped into the light.

CHAPTER EIGHT

The Portents of War

"There is a war coming."

Emma studied the faun under the daylight. Tattoos covered his skin. Sinuous lines and shapes snaked all over his body except where there was fur. His face was lined with age. Bushy eyebrows, a long nose, and a protruding chin dominated his features. Dark, deep-set eyes looked back at Emma, their strangeness unsettling her. The flute the faun carried with him was much longer than Emma's and, whereas hers was plain, the one belonging to Domino was elaborate. Rich carvings of animals decorated the smooth and polished instrument.

She sat cross-legged on the forest floor, looking up at the strange creature. Domino leaned against the great oak.

"There are two worlds, Emma," he said. "This one and the World of Light. Their fates are intertwined, as they have been for a very long time. In that other world there lives a great power. He rules there and waits for the time to strike. He plans to return to this world and make it his own again, like it was once before. He is coming, and this is only the beginning. He means to make war with this world and rule over it, and there is no one who can stop him but you."

The faun's voice was deep and musical. He spoke as though making a rehearsed speech. As she listened, Emma tried not to stare at his tattoos, but they shifted about ever so slightly. This did not help her unease.

"Me?" she said.

"You, Emma," he said. "So my friend has foretold." He motioned toward the tree. "The trees are older than all of us, and they understand far more about this world than we do. We all come from the trees. The trees all have names and purposes."

"What is his name?" Emma said.

"That is not for me to reveal. The tree may tell you his true name one day."

"I'll call him Mr Oak," she said.

Domino made an expression resembling a smile. It frightened her.

"I don't think I understand anything," she said. "I'm supposed to stop someone from taking over the world? Me? But how?"

Domino looked away. "I don't know," he said. "All I know is that only you can, and I do not know why or how. That is a mystery for another day, I suppose."

He sighed and crouched down next to her. "Emma," he said. "All stories are true. But the trees and the Lord of Light were here first. He ruled over this world once, and then he left to his World of Light. Now he seeks to return. Minotaur has a mission. He is the vanguard. He comes to prepare the way. The humans who have disappeared are the first prisoners of war."

"So they're alive?" Emma said. "Where are they? We have to tell everyone so they can be rescued!"

"No one can go where they have been taken, and no one can save them."

"How can they not be saved?"

"They are in another world," Domino said. "When you are ready, maybe the trees will send you there, but I do not know. First you must stop Minotaur.

"You must understand. They are coming back. Many of the creatures that once inhabited this world are returning. Every story you have ever heard, they are all true. Those creatures left this world long ago, but they are coming back, friend and foe alike.

"Minotaur grows ever stronger. He comes only at night and cannot leave the forest, for he is not yet permitted. But soon, the Lord of Light will unleash him upon the world and none will be able to stand against him and his army. What you must do, Emma, is defeat him before he gains the power to conquer the world for his master."

The vision of the minotaur was still vivid in Emma's mind. She recalled the monster, his size and power, and the fire in his eyes.

"How? How can I stop that thing?"

There was a long pause before Domino spoke again. "I do not know," he said.

"This is crazy," Emma said. "Are you sure you have the right person? How could it be me? Why is it me?"

"It is you, Emma. My friend, your Mr Oak, has affirmed it is so."

"I can't believe my dad would agree to this. He told me you would only teach me to defend myself!"

Domino nodded. "That is what he believes, and what I led him to believe. You must let him keep believing it. We have argued about this for years. Both he and I hoped this would not happen so soon, but no one can predict what the Lord of Light will do, not even the trees."

Emma's head was swimming. There was a whole other world she had been unaware of, and her father had known about it all along. What other secrets had he kept from her?

"So I'm supposed to stop a giant monster and save the world just because a tree told you so?"

Domino nodded.

"That doesn't seem right at all," Emma said. "I think there are things you're not telling me."

A hint of a smile crept across Domino's strange features. His eyes appeared to twinkle. "This is a brand new world for you, Emma," he said. "There will be many surprises to come."

The faun stood up. He offered his hand to Emma.

"Return to me every day from now on," he said. "Come alone. I will teach you the things you need to know. Go rest now. What is to come will not be easy."

As Emma walked home, it felt to her as though none of what had transpired had been real, as though it had happened to someone else, or as though it had been a dream. She felt exhausted with the weight of it all.

She had dreamt of saving the world like the heroes in her books did. She loved the stories about unlikely individuals destined for greatness. But all that the faun had told her seemed so much bigger than she was, and she did not understand half of it. She did not know if any of her heroes had ever been so plainly confused.

Her father was waiting for her just beyond the doorway to their house. She ran to him, hugged him tightly, and closed her eyes. She felt his arms wrap around her small frame.

She tried to speak but could only think of two words. "Why me?" she said.

Her father took her in his arms and carried her to the armchair. He sat down. Emma curled up into him.

"Do you know why Lucy came here last night, Emma? Did I tell you?"

"To snitch."

"No, Emma," he said. "Her parents have gone missing."

"Oh," Emma said.

"Lucy came here because she knew you were searching the forest. She said you were mapping it out, and she wanted to know if you'd found anything. She thought maybe your maps would help."

Emma recalled what the faun had said. The ones who were missing were in another world. They could not be saved.

"I can't help anyone, Dad."

"But that's the thing, Emma," he said. "Lucy believes you can, just like Jake believes you can help him. They believe in you because you are special."

"I'm not special," she said.

"Let me tell you a story," he said, "about the day you were born. It was the sunniest of days when you were born, my little girl. A beautiful day in April."

"April?" Emma said. "Dad, I was born in May!"

He chuckled. "I know, my dear. I'm just teasing you. It was a beautiful day in May. Will was just a toddler, a two-year-old hurricane of a kid. Grandma was taking care of him at her old house.

"I was there at the hospital when mom gave birth. It was a sunny day. The birds were chirping, welcoming you into the world. You were so little back then that I could hold you in one hand.

"You were so healthy, we brought you home right away. We drove back with the windows down. Mom was holding you in the car. Your little eyes were opened wide, and you were staring at everything in your new world, laughing at what you saw. That was the most beautiful sound, when I first heard you laugh.

"We were almost home—we were driving by the forest—when it happened. It was very quiet at first, but I slowed the car down, and we listened carefully. It only got louder."

"What was it, Dad?"

"It was the forest," he said. "The whole forest was singing to you and welcoming you home. It all started with a single tree. It started singing for you, and then the whole forest took up its song. The song was heard all over and no one could explain it, but we knew it was for you. This is how we know you're special, Emma. The forests sang to you on the day that you were born."

Emma smiled. She closed her eyes.

She woke up in her bed, still wearing her dirty pyjamas from the day before. She sat up groggily, not sure how long she had slept. A glance out the window told her it was still early afternoon.

"Did I dream everything?"

The flute on her nightstand attested she had not. She put it under the bed and went to her father's office.

"Hey, Emma," he said from his place at his desk. He turned his chair to face her and leaned forward. Emma could tell he had not slept all night. "How are you feeling?"

"Fine," Emma said. Her feet hurt. Despite the short nap, she felt tired still. Her mind raced, overwhelmed with thoughts of the faun in the forest and the things he had told her. There was another world, and it was making war with her own. Andrew Milligan was a prisoner. He could not be saved.

And now, Lucy's parents were missing.

"Dad," Emma said. "I think I need to apologize to Lucy."

He nodded. "I think you're right," he said. "We should check up on her. I'll call her while you get something to eat and clean yourself up."

Lucy Leroux's neighbourhood was located close to the University of Saint Martin. It was a neighbourhood of big houses, long driveways, and two-door garages. Lucy's house fit right in. It was a wide, two-story house dabbed generously with large windows.

They pulled into the driveway.

"Can I talk to her by myself?" Emma said. "Just to apologize. You can come in after."

"Sure, Emma," he said, switching off the car. He leaned back in his seat and closed his eyes.

Emma rushed to the front door. Lucy's lawn was littered with flower beds and well-maintained shrubs. Her door was painted a pure white and had a golden angel affixed to it. A little inspection revealed that the angel hung on a on swivel so it could be used for knocking. There was also a button beside the door, so Emma hesitated, unsure whether to use the button or the knocker.

The door opened before she could decide. Emma looked up at Lucy Leroux. The older girl's eyes were red. Her clothes were wrinkled.

"Hey," Lucy said.

"Hi, Lucy. Can I talk to you?"

Lucy glanced past her into the car in the driveway. "Is Professor Wilkins sleeping?"

"I think so," Emma said, looking over her shoulder. "He had a long night."

"Does he want to come in?"

"No, he's fine."

Lucy, looking dubious, stepped aside so Emma could enter. They went inside and sat down in an expansive living room. The furniture within was clean and orderly except for a couch which faced a big screen television. A box of tissues rested among a nest of blankets piled on its cushions.

"Sorry," Lucy said. "I kind of slept here."

"It's okay," she said, pausing when she saw movement inside the house. A striped cat had entered the room. He walked along its periphery, casting a glance at Emma now and then.

"I wanted to say I'm sorry," Emma continued. "I was very rude. I didn't know what had happened. I'm sorry. You're always so nice to me. I'm sorry, okay?"

"Don't worry about it," Lucy said. "I'm sorry too. I didn't know he didn't know about the forest. And I wasn't feeling right."

"What happened?"

"I don't know," Lucy said, looking out the window. "They just vanished. I talked to my mom and dad that morning before school, and then they were just gone when I came back. All their stuff is here, and the cars are in the garage. I don't know what's happening."

Emma did not know how much she could tell Lucy about what she had learnt in the forest. The girl would think her crazy if she told her everything. And maybe her parents were simply missing for another reason. Perhaps they had not been taken prisoner.

"What about your mom, Emma?" Lucy said. "I didn't see her the other day."

"She died when I was a baby. I don't even remember her."

The striped cat jumped up on Emma's lap. He glared at her for a moment, then strode off to sit on an armrest.

"Hello," Emma said to the cat.

"That's Sprinkles," Lucy said.

"Hello, Mr Sprinkles," Emma said and reached out to pet him.

"Don't you put a hand on me, foolish girl," Sprinkles said.

Emma withdrew her arm quickly. "I'm sorry."

"It's okay," Lucy said. "You don't have to apologize anymore, okay?"

"You didn't hear that?"

"Hear what?"

"Nothing," Emma said. "I'm just imagining things, I guess."

"Her sobbing has been worse than ever since the others went away," Sprinkles said. "That is what's wrong with the way they cling to one another..."

The cat rambled on.

Lucy started to speak, but Emma found it difficult to concentrate on her words due to the ramblings of the cat.

The older girl was saying something about her parents, as far as Emma could tell. Tears welled up in her eyes, and she wiped at them with her sleeve.

Sprinkles jumped off the couch and leaped to the windowsill, still rambling. "... fifteen years or more. It's no surprise they can't find their own way after all that time..."

"Please stop!" Emma said. Sprinkles fell silent. So did Lucy.

"No, I didn't mean you!" Emma said. "Sorry, I was... I'm sorry. I always end up being so rude to you. It's bad luck, I swear. I don't mean it."

Lucy wiped at her face again.

Emma, determined to set things right with Lucy, walked over to her couch and sat beside her on top of the blankets. She put an arm around the older girl. Lucy smiled faintly. Encouraged, Emma took her hand and squeezed it.

"Do you know what I do when I'm very sad?" she said.

"What?" Lucy said.

"I just cry a lot," Emma said.

At first, Lucy only frowned. But a moment later, her smile widened, and she broke into laughter. Sprinkles stopped pacing on the windowsill, sat down, and stared at them.

"So, listen," Emma said, "if you get very sad you can come over any time you want, and we can just cry together."

"Thank you, Emma," Lucy said, still smiling. "Are you sure you're eleven?"

"Pretty sure," she said.

"Maybe you're not so foolish, after all, foolish girl," Sprinkles said from the windowsill.

Emma shook her father awake.

"Sorry," he said. "I fell asleep. Is it time?"

"It's over, Dad," she said. "I went and talked to her."

He adjusted his glasses and turned the ignition. The car rumbled to life. "How is she doing?"

"Can she come live with us?" Emma said.

He raised his eyebrows. "What?"

"She's in bad shape, Dad," she said. "We could take care of her."

"Tell you what," he said. "We'll keep a good eye on her. She can come over anytime, and we'll check up on her often."

"Okay, Dad."

They returned home. Before Emma could get out of the car, her father spoke. "Here," he said as he removed a small, grey box from the glove compartment. "Someone left this in my office the other day. It's a present, I think, but I don't know who left it. I thought it would be good for you."

Emma opened the box, revealing a small, grey watch with a cartoon mouse on it. The mouse was grinning with big, white teeth and sticking out his thumb in a gesture of encouragement.

"Thank you," she said. "It's my favourite colour. I never had a watch before."

"I know," he said. "It's about time you did." He chuckled at that for some reason that Emma could not understand.

They went inside the house. Will was waiting for them. "Emma," he said. "I guess you're a superhero now or something?"

She smiled and punched him in the shoulder. She then hugged him tightly.

CHAPTER NINE

Mr Jingles

On Thursday morning, Emma returned to school. She passed Mr Clarence on her way into the school building. She put her head down, hoping he would not notice her. She had missed detention. There was a note in her backpack excusing her absence, but it was addressed to Ms Robins. Emma had forgotten about the principal.

She shuffled into the school among the other children from her bus and made her way down the hall, glancing over her shoulder just in time to see Mr Clarence pass through the doorway. She gulped. The principal was looking in her direction. Facing forward again, she made her way quickly to the stairwell and scampered up.

At the top of the stairs, she looked down. Mr Clarence stood at the foot of the steps. He glanced up at her and started making his way up. Emma sprinted to her classroom.

Ms Robins was not there yet. Taking advantage of her absence, children milled about in groups, chatting and laughing. Emma rushed to her seat and produced the note from her backpack, ready to deliver it to her teacher the second she walked in the door.

Jake arrived momentarily. He hurried over to her.

"So what happened?" he said.

Emma took a moment to contemplate. "Everything," she said finally, not sure where to begin. Somehow, she had to tell the boy the whereabouts of his father.

"Everyone have a seat."

Mr Clarence stood just inside the door. The children scrambled to their desks. The principal made his way to the front of the classroom.

"I'll tell you at recess," Emma whispered.

Jake nodded. He went to his seat.

"Since there were a couple of absentees yesterday," Mr Clarence said, "some of you may not know that Ms Robins is unable to teach at this time. I'll be taking over her teaching duties for today."

Emma and Jake exchanged a glance. She wondered if Ms Robins was yet another disappearance.

The morning wore on.

When the recess bell tolled, the children scrambled toward the door.

"Emma Wilkins," Mr Clarence said amid the commotion. "Please stay back a moment. I need to speak with you."

Emma stopped halfway up from her chair and sat back down. Mr Clarence had not forgotten about detention, it seemed. Maybe the note for her teacher would save her life this time. Since Mr Clarence was substituting for Ms Robins, it would be reasonable for Emma to give the note to him instead.

Jake looked back at her from the door. She shrugged and mouthed the word "lunchtime."

The boy nodded and left the room, leaving her alone with the principal.

"It won't be too long now," Mr Clarence said. "Have a seat over here, Emma." He motioned to a desk in the front row. Emma scurried over and sat down.

"Rebecca Robins has disappeared with the rest of them, you see," the principal said. "It won't be long now. Not long at all."

"Sir?"

He smiled. "The storm is coming, Emma. Very soon. No more than a week, perhaps. Time is running out."

Emma looked out the window. Outside, it was sunny.

"I suspect they will decide to close the school soon. And who knows what the reaction will be like out there." He swept his arm toward the windows.

Emma did not know what to say.

"I'm just a rambling old man," Mr Clarence said. He sighed. "I'll get to my point. You are very far ahead in your lessons, correct?"

"Yes, sir," Emma said.

"I think, then, that you should take the next few days off school to make time for your... extra-curriculars. I know you're very busy with certain projects."

"Yes, sir," Emma said. She was baffled.

"Time is running out, Emma, and these projects of yours are very important. You must hurry."

"I will, sir, Mr Clarence," Emma said. She did not understand what was happening. Did Mr Clarence know about the forest, or was he talking about something else entirely? Had he mistaken her for someone else? The principal had mentioned Ms Robins disappearing "with the rest of them." Did he know what had really happened?

He smiled. "Well," he said. "Now that that's done with, let's see what you got there." He approached the desk and took her hand. "Now that's a funny little watch, don't you think?"

"Yes, Mr Clarence," she said.

"But really look at it, Emma. Quite funny, isn't it?"

She looked down at the watch on her wrist and the little cartoon mouse. It really was a silly watch, she thought. The mouse was grinning a wide, toothy grin and giving a thumbs-up.

Dark, round eyes looked back at her. There was mirth in those eyes. Faint, cheerful lights fluttered about on the circular surfaces. They twirled around and chased after one another. The mouse waved. Emma waved back with her free hand, though she could not pull her eyes away from the happy lights. They were butterflies now, drifting in a warm breeze above a green meadow. Beyond the meadow, past a lazy, blue river, there stood a great forest. Tall trees, vibrant green, reached up to the blue sky toward a yellow sun. They swayed in the wind.

The mouse's grin widened. He laughed cheerfully, hands on his grey, round belly, almost doubling over. Emma giggled.

The chime of the school bell startled her. Children streamed in through the classroom door. Mr Clarence, sitting on Ms Robins' chair, thumbed through a stack of papers.

Emma shook her head. She remembered Mr Clarence had asked her to remain behind at the start of recess. She could not recall the events between then and now. She tried to concentrate. Nebulous images resolved into memories. Mr Clarence had told her to stay home from school because there would be a storm. Then something had happened to her watch.

She looked at her wrist. The watch was intact and exactly as it had always been. The grey cartoon mouse looked back at her with his toothy grin. He held up his hand as he always had: five fingers spread out as though waving to her.

It was lunchtime at Wizard Falls. Emma told Jake

everything that had happened to her in the last two days. She told him of the minotaur and the faun; of the great oak in the forest; of what Domino had told her about a coming war.

"So you know where my dad is?" Jake said.

"Well, no," she said. "Okay, yes. Sort of. This minotaur thing took him, is what I understand, to another world, somehow."

"To the world where the bad guy lives?" he said.

"The Lord of Light," Emma said. "I know nothing about him. But yeah, he's coming to take over the world. But the minotaur is here to take over the world first, or something like that, and I'm supposed to stop him. But I don't know how, and neither does the faun."

Jake frowned. "It's very confusing," he said. "So you're supposed to save the world because a tree said so?"

Emma nodded. "Mr Oak."

"And what about the prisoners?"

"Domino said if I stop the minotaur, then maybe the trees will send me to the other world to save them."

"So you might have to leave?" Jake said.

Emma sighed.

The sun was high in the sky. Warm light bathed the ring of trees that surrounded them. It glinted off the rivulet that coursed lazily nearby. The gentle trickle of water behind them crooned a delicate lullaby. At that moment, she wished she could close her eyes and stay there for a long, long time.

"I'll do anything to find your dad," she said. "Trust me, Jake."

The boy took her hand in his. She leaned her head against his shoulder. They said nothing more until it was time to go back to school.

It did not take long for Emma to find the oak's glade that afternoon. She went to the forest alone, just as Domino had instructed. A short, aimless stroll brought her within sight of the clearing. It was as though it had come to her. Brown-green leaves crowned the great oak at the glade's centre, even though the ring of trees surrounding it was ablaze with autumn colours.

Emma entered the clearing holding her flute in hand. Domino was nowhere to be seen. She approached the oak and placed her hand against him, feeling his warmth, listening to his soft melody.

"Hello, Mr Oak," she said. "My dad told me you and the forest sang to me when I was born. I think he just made up the story though."

"He has been watching over you all your life."

She had not heard Domino arrive. The faun stood close behind her. "As have I," he continued. "I've watched and waited for him to signal that you were needed, that you were ready. We know the former is true, but I'm not sure about the latter."

Emma turned to face the faun. "So you don't think I'm ready?"

Domino spread his arms and bowed slightly.

"The Lord of Light has made his move a lot sooner than expected."

"Well, I don't think I'm ready either. How am I supposed to do this? What makes me different from anyone else? This thing," she said, waving the flute around, "does it do anything? Is it like a magic wand?"

Domino shook his head. "It is not a magic wand," he said. "That is a weapon for another story."

"Then what does it do?"

"That is what I will teach you," he said. "If you stop asking questions for a moment."

"Sorry."

"We all come from the trees," Domino said. "From the trees comes the music. It is in all of us, even in those who have forgotten it. You can understand animals now, but that is not a special ability. The animals communicate using the music still, and anyone could understand if only they would listen. When you passed through the light of the tree, he compelled you to remember. You learnt to do it once again."

"But they can't understand me," Emma said.

"No, they cannot. You learnt how to listen, but you do not know how to speak."

"Do I have to play this?" she said, wiggling her fingers about the flute.

"If you like," he said. "It is a worthwhile pursuit." He brought his own flute to his lips and played a short melody. "But what this instrument produces is only a part of the music. The music that travels through the air as sound is but a subset of the true music."

Emma pursed her lips. "I'm confused."

"The part you hear is not the whole. There is a hidden part humans cannot hear... nor see, for it is also light."

"I think I understand," she said. "Not really, but sort of. It still doesn't tell me what the flute actually does, though."

The faun made a short, wheezing sound. Emma thought it resembled a strange, alien sigh.

"The flute takes the music from inside you and amplifies its power. This power can be used to communicate farther than you ever could on your own, or it can be used for violence. First, you must learn to use this power to speak, and then you will learn to use it for other purposes."

The faun drew her away from the tree and close to the edge of the clearing. He gazed into the forest. A faint glimmer surrounded his flute. Shortly after, there was a great rustle of brush as a herd of rabbits, a dozen or more, crashed into the clearing.

It took a moment for Emma to see it. They were not rabbits, at least not normal ones. On each of their little heads, between their ears, there grew a small set of antlers.

The animals noticed Emma and dashed to surround her. A chorus of little voices greeted her:

"Miss Emma!"

"Hello, Miss Emma!"

"Welcome, Miss Emma!"

Emma could not help herself. She burst into laughter and knelt down to pet them. They overwhelmed her. She found herself on the ground with a flurry of the little beasts dancing around her and over her.

"Jackalopes," Domino said. "Friendly, forgiving, and playful. They are the perfect creatures for helping you learn."

The faun leaned down and picked up a jackalope. He scratched the animal's chest. The little creature settled into his arms in delight.

"Settle down for a moment," Domino said, raising a hand. The jackalopes withdrew their attack on Emma. They gathered around the faun, sitting back on their haunches. Emma stood up.

"Bucks and does," Domino said to the assembly of jackalopes. "You are here to help Emma learn to speak."

An excited commotion surged among the critters. Domino quieted them down with a wave of his hand. He put down the jackalope he had been holding. The little animal skipped to Emma and sat down by her side.

"Hello," Emma said.

A high, chirping sound emerged from the herd of jackalopes.

"They are laughing," Domino said. "They think you are saying nonsense. Try saying something else."

"Okay," Emma said sheepishly. "Nice to meet you, bucks and does."

More laughter followed. This time, it was up-
roarious. Some jackalopes danced around in little
circles. Others slapped at the ground with a hind
paw. Two or three even wiggled around on the
ground, their soft bellies facing the sky. Apologies
accompanied the laughter:

"Sorry, Miss Emma!"

"Can't help it, Miss Emma."

"You're so funny, Miss Emma."

Domino, smiling at their glee, allowed them their
mirth for a moment. He then raised his hand
again. The pandemonium abated, however slowly.

"Music is light, Emma," he said, "and light is
music. Sit down over here next to me and close
your eyes."

She sat where he indicated. They faced the jackalopes, who were assembled as an audience. She
closed her eyes.

"Concentrate," Domino said. "Breathe deeply.
Focus on your breathing and only your breathing.
Feel the air flowing into you. It is a gift from the
trees. Feel the air flowing out of you. It is what
you are giving back. In this way you are connected
physically, perpetually, to the world and all its inhabitants."

Emma breathed in the cool forest air. She knew
the faun was talking about the oxygen cycle.
Maybe this would be easier than she thought. She
remembered the diagram showing oxygen coming
out of a tree and going into a little horse who released carbon dioxide, which—

"Concentrate!" Domino said.

"How do you know I'm not?"

"You are grinning like a fool who believes she knows everything."

A murmur of hushed laughter buzzed through her audience.

"Let us try again," Domino said.

The faun repeated his speech. Emma breathed in and out. This time, Domino guided her. His deep voice whispered close to her and kept her on task, prompting her every inhalation and exhalation. At first, it was difficult to keep her thoughts from intruding. In mid-breath, she would think about Jake, wondering what he was doing. She would think about how strange her life had so suddenly become. When she banished these thoughts, when she thought she had her mind under control, she would think of the minotaur and the coming war.

"Focus, Emma," Domino whispered. "Do not try to think of nothing. Instead, focus on the gift from the trees until the rest fades away."

She complied, fixating her mind on her breathing. Cool air entered through her nose, coursed down into her lungs, and came back out through her mouth. She took what the trees had given, and she gave something back. Endlessly, the gift from the trees travelled through her, a constant, life-giving stream flowing in and out of her body.

Emma lost track of time. The clearing fell away and dissolved into nothingness. Her world became darkness. All that existed was the mesmerizing thrum of Domino's voice.

"There is a light inside you, Emma," the faun said. "Deep within. Faint and frail. Find it."

Emma drifted alone in a black universe. She was a vessel. A single spark of light, feeble and minuscule, flickered inside her.

"Good," Domino said. "This is your voice. Use it. Speak now!"

"Hello," Emma said. The spark of light flared up for a brief instant.

A sudden clamour erupted. Emma's eyes snapped open.

The jackalopes jumped about in delight, cheering, whooping. Appreciative laughter accompanied their little voices:

"Hello, Miss Emma!"

"You did it, Miss Emma!"

"Way to go, Miss Emma!"

The jackalopes charged straight at her. Soon she was on the ground again, a dozen little critters swarming all around her. Her laughter filled the clearing.

So the afternoon wore on for Emma and the jackalopes. Domino guided her through the same exercise repeatedly. The enthusiasm of the jackalopes was encouraging, and it never abated, though Emma grew tired as the shadows lengthened.

Domino noticed her weariness. "That will be enough for today," he said. "Learning to use the light can be exhausting. I have pushed you hard because we have little time. You must practise what you have learnt at every opportunity."

He dismissed the jackalopes. Emma waved to the critters as they bounded away, chirping their goodbyes:

"Bye, Miss Emma!"

"Goodnight, Miss Emma!"

"See you again, Miss Emma!"

Emma did not notice her new companion until she was back on Belle Street. A jackalope loped alongside her. Dark brown eyes, each surrounded by a ring of white fur, looked up at her. The critter's coat was thick, brown, and mottled with small, white patches. Upright ears swivelled back and forth, flanking the miniature set of antlers that sprouted from the animal's head.

"Hello there," Emma said, then remembered that the jackalope did not understand her. To properly speak to the creature, she would have to sit down and perform the exercise Domino had taught her. She stopped walking and pursed her lips, wondering what to do.

The jackalope sat up on its hind legs. "Let's go home," it said.

"Home?" Emma said. She pointed toward the forest. The jackalope shook its little head. "Not there? Where is home then?"

The creature tapped a paw on the rough asphalt. "Home!" it said, impatiently.

"Home? Do you want to come to my house? Is

that it?"

She shrugged and resumed walking. The jackalope followed.

Upon arriving home, they found Will and her father sitting at the dinner table. Will's chair scraped the floor as it slid back. He stood up quickly and rushed over to them. Her father followed, the trace of a smirk raising the corner of his mouth.

"There you are," he said. "Who's your friend?"

"Are those antlers?" Will said.

"This is a jackalope," she said. "I don't know its name, or if it's a boy or girl. It sounds like a boy, though."

Will bent down to pet the animal. "This is unbelievable," he said. "You didn't glue these on, did you?"

William Wilkins smiled at the jackalope. He squatted down and scratched behind the critter's ears. The jackalope closed its eyes and stretched its neck contentedly, pawing at the carpet.

"You must be hungry," William said. "Let's go sit down. Is your friend hungry?"

"I suppose," Emma said. "But I don't know what it eats."

She went to the refrigerator and waved the jackalope over. It obliged and skipped to her. She poked around in the vegetable drawer.

"Do you like Brussels sprouts? Broccoli? Kale?"

She filled a plate with vegetables, tearing or cutting them into small pieces, and placed it on the floor for the jackalope.

"Thank you, Miss Emma," the jackalope said and began to eat.

Emma took her seat at the table.

When the meal was over, she went down to the basement and searched through their Christmas boxes. She dug through them until she found a small Santa hat that had belonged to her when she was younger. It was big for her purposes, but she made adjustments to it using her scissors, a needle, and some thread from her yellow lunch box.

When she finished, she put the hat on the jackalope's head, covering its little antlers. The hat bulged awkwardly, but the antlers held it in place. There was a little bell at the tip of the hat. It jingled whenever the jackalope moved around.

"I think you're a boy," Emma said. "I don't know your name, so I'll call you Mr Jingles for now. We'll pretend you're my pet rabbit when anyone's around."

Emma, somewhat re-energized by her meal, spent the rest of the evening in her bedroom practising what Domino had taught her, finding the light and using it to speak to Mr Jingles. Her progress was slow, but the jackalope seemed happy to help. He bounced around the bed whenever Emma uttered so much as a simple "hello." The process was tiring, but she fought against her fatigue, remembering what Domino had told her. She had to practise at every opportunity.

At some point in the night, Emma's tired eyelids

would not stay open. She put her head down on her pillow.

Mr Jingles ambled over and nestled against her chest.

Emma smiled drowsily. She put her arm around the jackalope, and then they both slept.

CHAPTER TEN

Dinner and a Unicorn

E mma opened her eyes. A fluffy white tail twitched before her. Jingles lay flat on his back, curled up, arched paws facing the ceiling. She yawned and checked the time on her watch. The grey mouse held up four fingers, as he always had. It was still early.

She stood up. Jingles stirred on the bed.

"Good morning, sleepy," she said.

The jackalope blinked several times. He then flipped over and jumped off the bed gracefully.

They went to the kitchen. Emma fixed a plate of vegetables for the jackalope—a carrot, chopped red pepper, and romaine lettuce—and filled a bowl with water before she set about making breakfast for her family.

The smell of food brought her father and her brother out of their bedrooms and into the kitchen.

"What's the occasion?" William said.

"I don't know," Emma said. "Well, I do. Dad, my principal, Mr Clarence, he said I shouldn't go to school for a few days. That I should take some time off. I'm not sure what he was talking about, something about a big storm, but I think it's probably a good idea with all that's going on, and I need to practise—"

"Absolutely not," he said. "How could you even consider that? Why would he suggest it? What kind of principal is this man? There is no way you're missing school."

"But, Dad, it's like the end of the world or something!"

Her brother opened his mouth. Before he could speak, William cut him off.

"No, Will, you can't skip school either. You're both going even if the world is burning."

After breakfast, Emma took Jingles out to the backyard.

"You can't come with me to school," she said. "You can stay here and wait for me, or you can go back to the forest if you like."

The jackalope tilted his head one way, then the other.

"You can't understand me, that's right."

Emma pursed her lips. If she took the time to speak to him using the light, they would be there all day and she would miss her bus. It took her far too long to say even one word, much less a whole sentence. There had to be another way to communicate with the jackalope. She recalled a story about a gorilla who had learnt sign language. The problem was that she did not know sign language. She did, however, know how to point.

Emma pointed at the jackalope and then to the surrounding yard. She then pointed at herself and walked in place.

"A guessing game, Miss Emma?" Jingles said.

She nodded vigorously, surprised that the jackalope knew about guessing games. But then she remembered, from her favourite book, that riddles were an ancient tradition among all peoples.

"Let's start again," she said.

Emma pointed at the jackalope and then straight down at the ground.

Jingles lay down.

She shook her head. Maybe she would miss her bus, after all.

Emma missed her bus.

But Jingles had eventually understood what she had been trying to say. He had stayed in the back-yard to wait for her return. Because she had been late for the bus, her father had been forced to drive her to school. She had made him late as well.

"Don't forget Lucy is coming for dinner tonight," he said, as they pulled up at the drop-off area in front of the school.

"She is?"

"Yes, Emma. I told you during dinner last night.

We said we would keep her close and look after her, remember? I called her while you were training in the forest."

"I'm sorry, Dad. I don't remember. I was really tired last night."

She pushed the car door open. "Emma," he said. "I am reminding you because I would like you to be on time for dinner. This means you might have to cut your lessons short."

She wanted to say that her lessons about saving the entire world were probably very important, maybe even more important than dinner, but she remembered that her father thought she was learning only self-defence.

"Can Jake come?" she said instead.

"Of course, Emma."

"Thank you!" she said. "I'll ask him!"

She leaped out of the car, shut the door, and turned to run.

When she arrived at her classroom, her face flushed from the sprint up the stairs, a wiry man wearing wire frame glasses turned from the chalkboard to look at her. He raised his eyebrows.

Jake waved at her slowly. The rest of the class stared.

"Where's Mr Clarence?" she blurted.

The thin man's eyebrows rose even more. "Who?"

He looked toward the Strike Board at the side of the classroom and then back toward Emma. "Ah," he said. "I assume you're Miss Wilkens. Please take your seat, Miss Wilkens."

"Yes, sir," Emma said dejectedly. She shuffled over to her desk.

The substitute teacher turned back to the chalkboard and resumed his lesson.

During morning recess, Emma headed down to the administrative area of the school. She approached the principal's office and noticed the door was closed despite his promise that it would always be open to her. She knocked on it and tried to turn the doorknob. It was locked. There was no response from within.

"Mr Clarence?" she said, knocking again.

A voice called out from down the hall. "Hello?" someone said. The voice was coming from the school's main office. Emma made her way there and poked her head around the doorway. Inside the office, a grey-haired woman stood behind a counter.

"Excuse me," Emma said. "Could you tell when I could see Mr Clarence?"

The woman raised an eyebrow. "Who?" she said.

"The principal," Emma said. "Mr Clarence."

The woman blinked. "Clarence?" she said, "My dear, I've been here for thirty years..." She paused as a faraway look came over her features. For a moment, there was a faint smile on her lips, but she shook her head and it disappeared. Finally, she spoke again. "Sweetie," she said, "there has never been a Mr Clarence here."

Emma suddenly felt dizzy. Her mind reeled. The floor beneath her tilted this way and that. She struggled to maintain her footing. Eyes wide with shock, she held on to the doorway to steady herself.

"But—" she said. No more words would come out.

The woman behind the counter stared at her, her face a composed, unreadable mask. For a moment, they only looked at each other.

Then the woman chuckled.

"I'm sorry," she said. "I'm just playing with you, little Miss Wilkins. Oh, my goodness, your reaction… I do hope you'll forgive me."

"Oh," Emma said, still reeling.

"George—Mr Clarence, I mean, has gone away on a family emergency. Don't you worry. He will be back before you know it."

"Oh," Emma repeated. The floor was only now beginning to settle.

"Are you okay, dear?"

"Oh. Yes," Emma said. "Thank you, Ms uh…"

"Call me Dory."

"Yes, Ms Dory."

After school, Emma found Jingles taking a nap under the shade of the cherry tree in her backyard. She sat down beside him. Momentarily, the jackalope opened his eyes and bolted up. He jumped onto her lap and nuzzled her chest.

"Hi, Mr Jingles," she said, giggling, "I'm sorry I had to leave. I hope you had a good day."

She held the jackalope in her arms for a little

while, brushing back his fur and feeling the texture of his antlers. They were velvety smooth, covered in short, fine fur.

She put him down on the grass and stood up.

"We have to go see Domino now," she said.

Together they set out toward Glenridge Forest.

Halfway down Belle Street, they came upon a little dog with big ears. Emma was alerted to his presence by a long, sharp howl. When she turned her head toward the source, she saw the dog standing on a porch in front of a small house across the street.

The dog sauntered over to them.

"A beagle," Emma said, delighted. "Hi, boy!"

The beagle ambled right up to the jackalope. His tail wagged furiously.

"Good day to you, sir," Jingles said.

The beagle tilted his head. "Hi, mister," he said. He nosed the jackalope and then sniffed him all over. When he was satisfied with his inspection, he licked his antlers. Then, slowly, the beagle opened his mouth wide and wrapped his teeth around one of the jackalope's tines.

"Please don't do that!" squeaked the jackalope.

The beagle backed off, seemingly bashful, big ears drooping nearly to the ground. "Sorry," he said. "Have you seen any squirrels? Or a cat, maybe? There is a cat that comes from that house down yonder and sits under the car, but I always chase him off."

"No," Jingles said. "No cats today."

"Okay, goodbye," the beagle said. He turned and strolled away toward his porch.

Emma and Jingles resumed their walk toward the forest.

"It appears he has fallen in love with you," Domino said upon seeing Emma and Jingles enter the clearing.

Emma smiled. She crouched and pet the jackalope behind the ears. Jingles clicked his teeth in pleasure. His fur was warm. It made a pleasant contrast to the cool air surrounding them. The sun was bright in a clear sky, but a chill breeze snaked around the trees of the forest and into the glade.

"Come over here," Domino said. He led her under the shadow of the great oak, right up to the tree's vast trunk. "Sit down with him."

She sat cross-legged with her back to the ancient oak. The tree was warm. Its undulating heat rippled against her back and flowed into her, filling her from head to toe. The pulsating warmth had a rhythm. It was like a song—or the beginnings of a song. It felt as though the oak was trying to tell her something, but she could not understand it. Not yet.

"Domino," Emma said. "You said that the missing people are in another world. But how does the minotaur get them there?"

"This tree has a twin," Domino said. "In another place in this forest."

"But why would a tree help him?"

"The trees all have their own identities and their own motives," Domino said. "No one truly understands why they do the things they do, not even the Lord of Light. They are not with or against him, but only do what they will. Not all the trees can make portals. In this forest there are only two: this one and his twin. Many of their brothers and sisters who once could are now dead."

"Because of us?"

Domino nodded. "Because of you," he said. "There will come a time, if we do not stop him, when the Lord of Light will return. He will come through here because here lies his portal of old, and this ancient tree and his brother will open for him it once again."

"But I thought Mr Oak wanted to help me stop him."

"He does," said Domino. "And he will. And when the time comes, he will help open the portal for the Lord of Light."

"That's very confusing."

"It is the way of the trees."

Emma frowned. She looked up into the leaves of the great oak and watched them dance in the breeze.

"Why can't we chop down the other tree? Wouldn't that stop him?"

"I think you would find that to be impossible, at least by normal means. This tree and his twin are not like the others. They exist here at this moment in time, but they go where they will. Come now," he said, motioning with his flute. "We have work to do."

Domino took her to the edge of the clearing. Jingles remained behind, nestled between the roots of the oak, eyes closing sleepily.

"I will now teach you to call the creatures of the world," the faun said. "To reach them from afar, you will need the aid of your flute. You must become a vessel of light, and the flute must become an extension of you through which the light will flow."

"Like a teapot!"

The faun laughed. It was a rich, strange sound. "Yes," he said. "Like a teapot."

He instructed Emma to close her eyes and become a vessel for the light. Emma breathed slowly and deeply, just as she had been practising. Time slipped away. Darkness enveloped her. For a while, she floated in space, alone and empty, a hollow vial. Then the light sparked to life inside of her.

"All stories are true," said the faun. "Do you know of Cerynitis? The Golden Hind? She now inhabits this forest. You must know her name if you are to call her."

When Domino spoke next, his voice was music. "Cerynitis," he said. The spark inside Emma danced in response. She saw the creature in her mind's eye. It was like looking at the wind. She saw golden antlers in flight, propelled by bronze hooves.

"Raise your hand, Emma," Domino said. His voice had returned to normal. "Call to her."

"Cerynitis," Emma said, urging the light inside of her to dance. The spark fluttered about for a moment, then it flared up and filled her. She directed the light toward the flute in her outstretched hand. The word, the light, exploded into the world.

As she said the word, she felt a gust of wind. She opened her eyes and saw the creature, the Golden Hind, standing before her: a great deer, tall and proud, with hooves of bronze. Resplendent antlers made of gold shone in the sunlight that filtered through the forest canopy.

Emma reached out to touch her. But suddenly, the creature was gone. It was as though Cerynitis had vanished, leaving no trace except for the gust of her departure.

Emma looked to the faun. Domino was staring straight at her. His eyes were wide.

"How did you do that?" he said. "Your voice... it was everywhere." He shook his head briskly and backed a step. "I must leave now. I do not know what you have done."

Emma looked at her watch. They had not been in the clearing for very long. When she looked back up, the faun had already left. She sighed, hoping she had not done something wrong. But the faun's reaction had been alarming.

At least she would be on time for dinner. Her father would be happy. Besides, the mouse on her watch still held up four fingers. It was still early.

Lucy arrived an hour before dinner time.

Emma was in her bedroom with Jingles when she heard a knock at the door. She took the Christmas hat from her bedside table and put it on the jackalope's head to conceal his antlers. The two of them rushed out to greet Lucy.

"Hey, Emma," Lucy said as she entered.

Emma's father closed the front door behind the visitor. Lucy's clothes looked as though she had slept in them. Dark, messy hair framed mournful, downcast eyes, though they brightened slightly upon seeing the jackalope.

"And you!" she said. "Hello, little guy or girl?"

"It's a boy," Emma said. "His name is Mr Jingles."

"Hello, Mr Jingles," Lucy said. She knelt.

"Good evening," Jingles said. Sensing her mood, the jackalope scurried close to the girl and nudged her leg with his nose. Lucy scratched the side of his neck. Jingles clicked his teeth happily.

Emma held her breath, hoping Lucy did not think to look under the hat, question its irregular shape, or wonder how it stood straight up on the jackalope's head. Maybe, she thought, the hat had been a silly idea.

Lucy stood up. "He just walks around like this? No cage or anything?"

"He's well trained," Emma said.

William Wilkins motioned toward the living room. "I'll start dinner," he said. "You two have a seat. Would you like something to drink, Lucy?"

"No, thank you, professor."

Half an hour later, there was another knock at the door. Emma jumped from her seat, eyes lighting up.

"That must be Jake!" she said.

"Is that your boyfriend?" Lucy said.

"No. He's just a friend," Emma said, flustered. She tried to wipe the smile from her face but found herself unable to do so.

Lucy, noticing her embarrassment, winked at her. "Yeah, he's your boyfriend," she said.

Emma shook her head, but her smile widened involuntarily. A second knock at the door saved her from further discomfiture.

She rushed to the door and opened it. Jake was not alone. His mother stood beside him.

"Oh, hello, Victoria Mrs Milligan," Emma said.

"Just Vicky, please, Emma," she said. "Hello, dear. Is your father home? He must be, right? I hope he doesn't mind that I stop by unannounced like this. I got home and straightaway Jake says he's coming over, so I thought I'd stop by to talk with your father. I hope it's not a problem. My dear, why is your face all red? Have you been running?"

"It's no problem at all," William said from the kitchen. He approached Victoria Milligan, hand outstretched. They shook hands. He invited the visitors inside.

"This is Lucy Leroux," he said. "She's one of my students. Lucy, this is Emma's friend Jake and his mother, Victoria Milligan." The jackalope hopped across the room to inspect the newcomers. "And this is Emma's pet rabbit."

Jake glanced toward Emma. She nodded.

"Dinner is almost ready," William said. "Please have a seat and get acquainted. Emma, come help me in the kitchen for a moment, please."

Emma checked the roast in the oven while her father mashed potatoes.

"How much do they know?" he asked quietly.

"Lucy knows nothing, Jake knows everything, and his mom knows something in between, probably. I don't know what Jake told her."

She shut the oven door and peeked over the kitchen counter. Jake sat on the couch next to his mother. Lucy sat on the couch across from them. Next to Lucy sat Mr Jingles, for all appearances taking part in the conversation.

"All right," William said. "Let's keep it quiet then."

The front door swung open. Will strode in and put his backpack in the closet next to the door. He turned and greeted the visitors.

"How was basketball?" William asked him from the kitchen.

"Good," Will said. "Joey broke his arm, but we won."

Emma went about setting the table. Plates rattled together. Forks and knives flew out from their drawers. Glasses clinked noisily against one another. Napkins lunged into place.

When everything was ready, they all sat down at

the dinner table. William Wilkins sat at the head of the table facing Victoria Milligan. Emma and Jake sat together. Across from them, Will and Lucy filled out the remaining places.

"The roast looks delicious, Professor Wilkins," Victoria said.

"Thank you," he said. "Just call me William, please."

As they ate, the adults did most of the talking. Emma's father and Jake's mother took turns interrogating Lucy about her studies and plans for the future. Will remained silent, busy shovelling food into his mouth. Emma and Jake sat close together and whispered.

"Can I see his antlers?" Jake said. He watched as Jingles munched on a bowl of vegetables in the corner.

"For sure," Emma whispered. "We'll sneak out to my room after dinner and I'll show you."

Jake smiled. "Great!" he said. Then a troubled expression took over his features. "Emma, when can I come back to the forest with you? When can I meet the faun and the tree?"

"Jake, I'm sorry," she said. "Domino says I have to come alone or he won't teach me."

"Oh," Jake said. He turned toward his food. They ate in silence for a while.

After dinner, they all moved back to the living room. William brought each of them a slice of cheesecake. He poured coffee for himself and Victoria Milligan.

"Lucy tells me her parents are missing," Jake's mother said.

"Yes," William said. "Very unfortunate."

"Funny that both her and Jake are friends with Emma," Victoria continued. "You know, Jake here has been telling me some crazy stories. I know they can't be true, but he thinks you know something about all the missing people."

"Mom, come on," Jake protested.

"No, it's all right," William said. "Well, what are these stories? Maybe we can clear things up for you, Victoria."

"Oh," she said. "Crazy things Jake talks about. Monsters and magic things. He said there is a minotaur in the forest and he's the one capturing people, and that Emma knows where all the missing people are. That can't possibly be true, can it?"

"Well, no, of course not," he said.

"But you know kids, Professor Williams—"

"Just William."

"William. They believe things, and Jake has his hopes up that his father can be found, by Emma no less, while the truth is far from that, and you can imagine how disappointed he will be."

"I see what you're saying," he said.

Emma was having a hard time keeping quiet. The last thing she would want to do was hurt Jake. She wanted to speak up and tell Victoria Milligan that it was all true. They were not just stories. She glanced at the jackalope curled up at her feet. She even had proof.

"Emma," William said, "has always had a great imagination. I'm sorry it has now caused trouble for you."

Emma stood up. She opened her mouth to speak. Her father shot her a look, frowning, and shook his head slightly.

"William," Victoria said. "I'm not sure how to put this gently. Jake and I are under a lot of stress with Andrew missing and my father ill. I'm not sure it's good for him to be hearing stories like that. I'm not sure he should really be friends with your daughter if—I'm sorry, I don't know how else to say it—if you can't control her."

Lucy stared down at her cheesecake, pretending she was not there. Will seemed on the verge of saying something. Jake's face was flushed.

"They're not stories!" Emma screeched. She reached down between her feet and took hold of Jingles' hat. Her father shook his head emphatically. His face was a mask of anger. He swallowed once, twice, then composed himself.

"Let me assure you," he said, turning back to Victoria Milligan, "Emma has no intention of hurting anyone and, while she may be telling stories, they are just that, even if, in moments of childish excitement, she may claim otherwise. You know how kids are with their imaginations. Emma loves books, especially fantasies. Elves and hobbits and all that. But she, generally, knows them for what they are: stories. They aren't real. They aren't true."

As though summoned by his words, on the road

outside, gloriously visible through the window, a magnificent white unicorn trotted by, its spiralling horn shining splendidly in the dying sun.

"Oh, my lord," Victoria Milligan said. Her mouth remained opened.

Lucy gasped.

"I told you it was true!" Jake said.

"Emma!" her father said. He nodded toward the front door.

She bolted outside. Jake followed her. They ran down the street, chasing after the creature. The unicorn trotted elegantly, glancing left and right as though taking in its surroundings.

They hardly gained any ground until the creature halted at the intersection of Belle Street and Glendale Avenue. He paused on the grassy shoulder before the road and stood observing the evening traffic.

Emma and Jake arrived panting.

She looked to the unicorn and then to the road. Cars were slowing down. Their drivers cast disbelieving stares toward the creature. Emma did not know what would happen if someone were to approach.

"We better do something soon," Jake said. "Can't you talk to him?"

"One word at a time," Emma said, "and it takes me a while to say it."

"I don't think we have a while," Jake said.

Heads had popped up at the windows of houses nearby. A few people had ventured outside to have a closer look.

Emma stood in front of the unicorn and closed her eyes, preparing to find the light and use it to speak to the creature. "What word, Jake?"

"I don't know!"

"Help me, Jake! What word?"

"Princess."

It was not Jake who had spoken. She opened her eyes.

"Princess," repeated the unicorn. "Greetings."

Emma shook her head. "Jake, I think he has me confused," she said. "This could work. He might let me ride him if he thinks I'm a princess. Help me up!"

"How do you know what he thinks?" Jake said.

"He told me."

"Oh. Of course." He frowned. "Wait. Have you ever even been on a horse?"

Emma shook her head. "Never."

Jake intertwined his fingers. Emma placed her foot on them. He lifted her up along the unicorn's flank. Her head did not even clear the creature's back.

"Higher, Jake!"

"I can't go higher!"

Suddenly, the unicorn lowered his body to the ground. He turned his head toward Emma and looked at her with one eye. "I am named Titanius, princess," he said. "I am honoured to be your steed. Where would you have me to take you?"

Emma climbed on the unicorn's back. Titanius

stood. She wrapped her arms and legs around him, clinging tightly.

"Be at ease, princess," Titanius said. "I will not let you fall."

Emma complied and sat back apprehensively. She raised her arm and pointed down Belle Street, back toward the forest. Without hesitation, Titanius turned and took flight. They became lightning.

The rest of the dinner party stood outside the Wilkins residence looking down the road. Some neighbours had also come out. Arnold Thornton, the biology professor next door, stood on his porch.

"Was that a horse?" Arnold said. "I heard hooves."

William shrugged. "I'm sure it was nothing out of the ordinary," he said.

A burst of lightning flashed before them. It happened only for an instant, but they saw it clearly. The great unicorn had passed by, crackling with electricity. He had been bearing a small girl on his back. The girl had looked just like Emma, but she had been wearing a long white dress that glittered in the twilight.

No one stirred until William Wilkins turned to face Victoria Milligan. "I suppose we have some explaining to do," he said.

He took them all inside and tried to explain everything.

Emma and Titanius arrived at Glenridge Forest. The run down the street had been a blur. Emma had fought the urge to bend down and cling to the unicorn, and Titanius had kept his promise. Riding him, despite their speed, had been effortless.

The unicorn slowed his pace when they entered the cover of the trees.

"Someone is here," Titanius said.

There was a sudden movement to their left. Emma turned just in time to see Domino drop to the ground from a tree. The faun was breathing heavily.

"Something is wrong," Domino said.

Titanius bent down. Emma jumped off him. She pointed toward the forest.

"Farewell, princess," Titanius said. "Until we meet again."

Emma and Domino watched him go. Lightning darted through the forest.

"Something is wrong," Domino repeated. "The forest is leaking. When you called Cerynitis, your cry was far stronger than I imagined it could be. Everyone heard it. They heard its power. And so the Lord of Light has made his move. Minotaur has been unleashed. A portal has been opened for his army."

"What does that mean?" Emma said.

"It means you are in danger. The world is in danger, and we have barely begun preparing."

"What can I do?" she said.

"Absolutely nothing," Domino said. "You can barely speak, much less fight. It is too late now. We have not so much as dreamt up a way to stop him. You must leave the forest. Go home, stay there, and wait for me. There are things I must attend to. There is no time!"

Domino leaped back into the trees. He disappeared into the woods.

"No time," she said to herself, frowning. There was something strange about the time. She looked at her watch. It was nearly seven-thirty. There was nothing strange about that. The grey mouse looked back at her, holding up three fingers as usual.

She shook her head, turned on the spot, and ran home.

CHAPTER ELEVEN

Invasion

Saturday. 9:00 a.m.

Phillip Matthews, Mayor of Saint Martin, sat at a table outside Marcy's Cafe, leafing through the pages of the local newspaper and sipping on a cup of black coffee. He wore a long scarf over his business suit. The weather had turned, and the morning was cool. There was little traffic on Main Street.

A black car pulled up in front of the cafe. From it emerged the man Phillip had been waiting for.

"Morning," the man said as he approached the mayor. He was a severe, grey-haired man whose nose hooked wickedly as though it had been broken many times in the past. Doug Peterson, Saint Martin's Chief of Police, sat down across the table.

"Good morning, Doug," Phillip said.

"I think we have a crisis in our hands," Doug Peterson said. "I have a plan, and I have people ready to do something about it. All I need is the go-ahead from you."

"Right to it then," said the mayor. "You're talking about the missing people."

Doug nodded. A young waitress came by the table and refilled the mayor's coffee. Doug asked for tea. He waited until the waitress had gone back inside before speaking again.

"There are more reports every day," he said. "We've been doing our best to keep it quiet, but you know how things get out. People are especially suspicious now that the construction site is closed."

Phillip sipped his coffee and looked out onto the street. Saint Martin had always been a quiet town, except maybe near the university. But even there, most incidents had amounted to nothing more than harmless nuisances. Kids being kids. Things had changed recently.

"You've heard these rumours about monsters, of course?"

"Of course," Doug said. "That's just people giving a face to their fear."

"What do we think is actually happening, Doug?"

"Gangs, maybe. Some psychos holed up in the forest. Cannibals. Maybe they come out to hunt for food."

Phillip chuckled.

"It doesn't matter who they are," Doug said. "We'll root them out in short order, and all this will be over and done with."

"So, Doug," Phillip said. "Indulge me for a moment. What if there really are monsters in that forest?"

"Cannibals, monsters, whatever they are," Doug said. "They're no match for a hundred armed officers."

10:37 a.m.

Lucy Leroux wandered around Penhurst Mall.

She walked past an ice cream shop near the food court. A woman behind the counter was watching her. It was the third time she had walked through that area.

Lucy was restless. The things she had learnt the day before had raced through her mind late into the night. She had awakened early. The story of the faun and the minotaur had bounded back into her mind as soon as she had opened her eyes. William Wilkins had said that her parents were in another world. She could hardly believe it, but she had seen the unicorn in plain sight. Emma had shown her the jackalope's antlers afterwards. Maybe anything was possible.

She turned toward the ice cream shop, intending to buy some small thing for appearance's sake —she had not been hungry in days. But then she heard a commotion from around the corner.

A crowd had gathered. It comprised, she guessed, maybe two dozen shoppers. They formed a wide semi-circle around a jewellery store. Many of them held up their cell phones, recording whatever was happening there.

Lucy heard yelling and the sound of breaking glass. She squirmed through a gap in the crowd.

She saw what she could only describe as goblins. They were short creatures covered in dirty, matted hair. They had long, pointed ears, bulbed noses, and sharp, fanged teeth.

The goblins romped about the store, breaking display cases, taking the jewellery from within, and thrusting it inside grimy sacks. Now and then, a goblin would hold up a ring or a necklace for the rest to see. The others would respond with grating sounds of admiration.

A befuddled security guard stood by while a well-dressed man, presumably the store supervisor, yelled in his ear and pointed furiously at the goblins.

Soon, the creatures had cleared out the place, leaving only empty shelves and broken glass. They rushed out of the shop and into the mall. The crowd scrambled to get out of their way.

The goblins dashed toward the nearest exit.

11:07 a.m.

Emma waited.

She had hardly slept. Domino had told her to

wait for him, and that was precisely what she had been doing. After the guests had all gone home the night before, she had alternated between sitting in her living room and pacing in the backyard with Jingles at her side. Sleep had finally overtaken her, and she had fallen asleep on the couch. She had woken up in her bed, wrapped up in a blanket, with Jingles snoring softly beside her.

Emma now paced about the living room, making slow circuits around the coffee table. She looked down at her watch. The grey mouse held up a peace sign, as though saying that everything would be all right. But it was already past eleven, and there had been no sign of Domino.

A knock at the door halted her pacing. Foreboding excitement made her heart race for a moment, but then she shook her head. It was unlikely that Domino would knock on the front door.

She rushed to the door and opened it. On the other side stood Lucy Leroux, her face flushed, breathing rapidly.

"Emma!" Lucy said. "I saw goblins at the mall!"

1:01 p.m.

Dorothy Welcher was watering her chrysanths when she saw the tiny man come strutting along the sidewalk. He looked oddly familiar, although he stood no more than three feet tall. He wore a red hat and sported a long, white beard. He marched swiftly, arms swinging wide at his sides, whistling a gleeful tune. His head turned this way and that as he went, taking in the neighbourhood.

When he saw Dorothy, he turned on the spot and came straight toward her.

Dorothy straightened as the little man approached. He tipped his hat and said something in a language she did not understand. She could only wave slowly, staring. The man's grin showed he was satisfied with that. He turned and walked away, now whistling again, but then something caught his eye.

Dorothy stood dumbfounded, realizing where she had seen him before.

The little man approached one of her garden gnomes. He poked the ceramic ornament with a fat finger. The garden gnome lurched precariously before falling over outright. A slight frown crossed the man's features, but then he tilted his head back in jolly laughter.

Dorothy forgot she was holding a watering can. It fell to the ground and splashed water all over her gardening boots.

The small man turned back toward her. He tipped his hat once more, said something that sounded apologetic, and then continued on his way down the street, whistling his cheerful melody.

4:56 p.m.

From beneath the shade of Glenridge Forest

emerged a fox. The dying light tinged her fur with streaks of gold. Keen ears erect, she raised her head to scent the air. Before the fox stood the grounds of the University of Saint Martin, quiet and idle.

Content the way was clear, the fox raced across a stretch of grass. A large building loomed beyond the field, and curiosity had the better of her. The building seemed made of glass. It blazed in the westering sun. Whatever the edifice was, it had the look of a place of power.

The fox dropped to the ground suddenly, sharp ears detecting the quiet grating of metal on metal.

To her right, a door had opened. Nearby stood a squat building, much shorter than her target, though comparably ample in breadth.

A group of young humans filed out, laughing and talking loudly. They strolled to the blazing structure and entered it casually, without ceremony.

The fox stood, her curiosity redoubled. She assumed human form and made her way to the glass structure, following the footsteps of the young humans.

7:49 p.m.

Madelyn Edinburgh put down her pen.

Sighing, she glanced at the stack of papers awaiting marking. They would have to wait until tomorrow. She picked up the stack and stuffed it into a briefcase.

Her desk was in disarray. She made a cursory

rearrangement of books, notes, and folders, then stepped out into the halls of the Harrison Walker Complex.

As she turned to lock her office door, she noticed a group of students approaching. This was not unusual for a Saturday night. Students would often go through the building, rather than around it, when returning to their residences after a meal or drinks in the commercial plaza across the street from the university grounds.

"Good evening," Madelyn said. The students did not respond. There was not so much as a glance in her direction. Their vacant eyes remained locked forward.

Madelyn shook her head as they passed. They were heading in the direction she intended to go. She stood in place for a moment to give them a head start. When they were a good distance away, she trailed behind them down the hall.

Once outside, the students turned to the right. Madelyn had expected them to go straight ahead and across the road on their way to the student residences. The direction they went led only to the old soccer field and, beyond it, Glenridge Forest.

Curiosity won her over. She followed, if only to see where they were going.

The students crossed the small service road that separated the lawns of the Harrison Walker Complex from the soccer field. Madelyn stopped just before the service road. She watched them cross the dark field under the light of a meagre moon.

They became only dark silhouettes as they neared the forest and disappeared almost entirely when embraced by its reaching shadows.

Madelyn frowned as her eyes adjusted to the feeble light. She could see the students, dark outlines against the darkness of the forest, but they were not alone. Dozens of other dark shapes surrounded them.

Her feet took her forward, almost unbidden.

The dark shapes were all students. Most of them stood motionless, facing the forest, but now and then one would break away from the group, enter the cover of the trees, and disappear into the darkness.

"What is happening?" she said loudly. No one so much as turned in her direction. She moved through the crowd. Vacant faces stared straight ahead as though unaware of her.

"Is this some sort of prank? What are you all doing?"

Again, no response.

Madelyn hesitated, wondering if she should call the police. Whatever was happening, even if it was only a prank, could not be good. Students were going into the forest after dark. The same forest where those construction workers had disappeared.

She walked away, pulling her mobile phone from her jacket.

But then Madelyn heard the music. A wave of warmth suddenly washed over her, and she understood then what the students were doing. They were listening.

The symphony enveloped her and filled her. It drove away all other thoughts. Her mobile phone fell from uncaring fingers. The briefcase at her side dropped to the ground.

Madelyn Edinburgh turned to face the woods and listen to the music of the forest.

8:10 p.m.

Arnold Thornton was driving home from dinner.

He did not notice it at first, as he drove toward The Hill, but when he approached Lockhart Road, it became obvious. An unusual number of people walked the streets of the city. Stranger still, they all seemed to be heading in the same direction.

He slowed as he approached the intersection. To his right, under the light of the street lamps, he saw a slow procession. It was a ragtag group walking loosely together: a grey-haired man supported by a cane; several young people, some teenagers, some a little older; a tall woman in a housecoat; a short man in pyjamas.

Arnold waited as they made their slow way across the street. They passed through the gleam of his headlights. He could see their faces. They all held the same vacant expression, eyes dead ahead. Once they had crossed, they turned onto Lockhart Road and walked along the grassy shoulder.

Arnold made his turn and drove slowly beside

them. He rolled down his window.

"Hey!" he said.

Blank faces stared straight ahead. Not one of them so much as blinked.

"What's wrong with you people?" he shouted. He blared the car's horn. No reaction. Agitated, he rolled up his window and stepped on the gas. Strange things had been happening lately. People had gone missing. The construction site had closed up suddenly. And then there was the white horse from the day before. Wilkins had rushed inside after that and said nothing to him, but Arnold was sure the rider had been William's daughter.

He drove on to the end of the row of houses along Lockhart Road. Glenridge forest rose to his left. A long line of people stood at the edge of the tree line, immobile, facing the forest. He squinted toward the woods, frowning, but could see nothing but darkness. He blared his horn once. Twice. Three times. No one moved, except for two or three who broke forward and ventured into the woods.

Arnold drove on. All along the length of the road, as far as he could see, it was the same sight. A mishmash of people of all ages stood at the side of the road before the trees, frozen, staring.

He shook his head as he turned down Belle Street, rushing to get home to call the police.

8:17 p.m.

Emma sat on floor of her living room with Jingles

dozing on her lap. The jackalope snored away. She had spent the day waiting for Domino. Lucy Leroux had waited with her until seven o'clock when she had gone home. Lucy had grown ever more distant as the day had wore on. Emma suspected the girl had been holding back tears.

Will and her father sat at the kitchen table. Her brother was reading a comic book. Her father was paging through a thick hardcover novel and listening to the radio. Neither of them had left the house all day as they waited for news from the faun.

Emma checked her watch. It was past eight, and still there had been no sign of Domino. The mouse on her watch was holding up his index finger. She frowned.

"Dad," she said. He looked up from his novel. "There is something weird about my watch."

"What is it, Emma?"

"I'm not sure," she said. "Just something strange —"

A sudden jolt ran through her.

"He's here!" she said.

"Who's here?" William said.

"Domino. He's calling me."

Emma stood up and ran out to the backyard. The faun was there. He stood just beyond the light that spilt from the house, under the shadows of the cherry tree.

"It has begun," Domino said. "It's too late. The Lord of Light has unleashed Minotaur. The trap is set."

William came up behind Emma.

"What did you say?" he asked the faun.

Domino shook his head slowly. "We've lost," he said. "It's over."

8:26 p.m.

Madelyn Edinburgh stood transfixed. The music of the forest was the most beautiful thing she had ever heard, and she never wanted it to stop. It was more than a symphony. It had flavour and scent and feel. She could almost see it sailing among the trees, veering this way and that, before dipping outside the forest and encircling her and all those around her.

No one moved, except for the few who sought the source of the music. Madelyn and most of the remaining congregation were satisfied with letting the symphony come to them. Perhaps later, Madelyn would follow. But not now. There was time. The forest had always sung. It always would.

Then the heavens fell.

The ground shook. Thunder erupted from the forest. Then a battering uproar, like a stampede of giants, rose alongside the music.

Madelyn's heart raced. Part of her mind screamed at her, telling her to flee. But the music would not let her. All she could manage was a slight turn of her head. Most of the students she could see stared blankly ahead, still listening, but panicked faces were peppered among them.

A young man turned and ran. Someone screamed.

The shadows of the forest thrashed about. The darkness itself bulged outward. Then it exploded.

Hulking creatures emerged from under the cover of the trees. They were creatures of legend: great trolls and orcs and centaurs and ogres. The creatures rushed forward, seized the students closest to them, and dragged them into the forest.

Chaos broke out.

She heard an earsplitting wail from above. Harpies circled the sky.

Many of the entranced broke out of their stupor. They tried to run, but more and more creatures poured out of the woods and ran them down. Those who struggled screamed as the beasts snapped their bones or tore at their flesh.

Madelyn stood immobilized, either by the music or by fear, she could not tell. A minotaur approached. He was the largest of all the creatures, towering over her as though she were a child. Blazing eyes glared down at her with fury.

The minotaur's hand wrapped around Madelyn's waist. He picked her up and threw her toward a passing centaur.

Sheer terror made her lose consciousness.

Sunday. 3:59 a.m.

Phillip Matthews woke up to the ringing of his mobile phone. He picked it up from the bedside table.

"Hello," he said, sitting up.

A distressed voice spoke for several minutes.

"Is this a joke?"

The voice assured him it was not a joke.

"Good heavens," Phillip murmured. "Set up an emergency meeting as soon as possible. Immediately. I will be in right away."

He hung up and then dialled Doug Peterson's number.

Laura Matthews stirred beside him. "What is happening?" she said drowsily.

"Trouble," Phillip said, shaking his head. He spoke into his phone: "Doug, how quickly can we move forward with your plan?"

Laura yawned. She rolled onto her side, away from Phillip, gathering the blankets around her body. "I hope it's nothing too awful," she said.

8:00 a.m.

Emma opened her eyes. She had fallen asleep.

Once Domino had spoken to them, he had rushed back out into the night. Her father had sent her to bed. She had not tried to sleep. Instead, she and Jingles had stayed awake as she had practised finding the light.

"There must be something more I can do," she had told Jingles. So they had worked at it late into the night. At some point, both exhausted, they had drifted off to sleep.

The jackalope lay beside her now, curled up against her. She placed a hand on his side and stroked his fur as she glanced out the window. The sky was gloomy. She could not guess how late she had slept.

She looked at her watch, remembering the eerie feeling it had given her the night before. The time was eight o'clock. The mouse on her watch was making a fist and scowling angrily. Something certainly was not right. Had the mouse always been like that? Why would her father give her a watch with an angry mouse on it?

She stood up just as Will poked his head into her bedroom.

"Emma!" he said. "Dad says to come see this!"

She followed him into their father's office. He sat at his desk watching something on his computer screen.

"Come look," William said as they entered. The siblings flanked their father.

A video played on the screen.

"For this reason I called an emergency meeting this morning," a man was saying. A caption identified him as Mayor Phillip Matthews. Near the top of the frame were the words: "State of Emergency."

"Last night," Phillip Matthews continued, "the City of Saint Martin suffered a terrible tragedy. Emergency lines are overloaded. We ask that you refrain from calling about missing persons.

"There have been reports of strange occurrences and disappearances everywhere throughout the city. There are, early counts show, hundreds of residents missing. The nexus of this activity appears to be Glenridge Forest.

"It is because of these circumstances I am now declaring a State of Emergency. Citizens are advised to stay home. Schools and public areas will be closed while we deal with this crisis.

"Please do not panic. You will be safe as long as you remain indoors. As we speak, a plan has been put into motion to find the missing persons and get to the bottom of this.

"We have put together a massive search party. They are armed, and they are gathering at the Paigely construction site as we speak. Federal aid is also on its way."

"What's going to happen, Dad?" Emma said.

"I don't know," he said. "Maybe we'll have to leave town, though that might only delay the inevitable." He shook his head. "This city will be overrun, starting with that search party, and then the next town and the next. Who knows where—"

The phone rang. William picked up a handset from his desk.

"Hello," he said. He turned the handset toward Emma. "It's Jake."

"Jake? Hello?" Emma said into the transmitter.

Jake's voice quivered. "Emma," he said, "my mom is gone."

CHAPTER TWELVE

The Lost

The streets of Saint Martin were nearly deserted. There were few cars on the road, and no pedestrians that Emma could see. She sat in the car's backseat, watching the houses flanking the road glide by.

"What are we going to do, Dad?" Will said from the passenger seat.

"I don't know," William said. He slowed the car down to pass an abandoned sedan. The vehicle sat in the middle of the road. The driver's side door hung wide open. "After we pick up Jake and Lucy, we'll have to sit tight. Wait for Domino to come back again."

"I don't understand, Dad," Emma said. "All we do is wait. Why can't I do something?"

Her father sighed. She could see his face in the rear-view mirror. Heavy eyelids and drawn features made it clear he had not slept.

"What can you do, Emma?" he said. "You've barely just started learning this... magic. We wait for Domino. He said this is only the beginning. He'll find out what happens next, and he'll think of a way to keep you all safe."

"Why do you trust him so much, Dad?" Will said. "How did you meet him?"

William sighed again. "I met him after Emma was born," he said. "He came to me after the forests sang for her."

"Is that really true?" Emma said. "Did the forests really sing?"

For a moment, her father said nothing. He opened his mouth to speak, but closed it again. "Of course it's true," he said finally.

They pulled up at a red light next to a minivan. The vehicle beside them was stuffed to the brim with luggage, clothing, and other odds and ends. A young woman sat in the driver's seat. A man next to her, on the passenger's side, held a small child on his lap.

"Dad," Emma said. "Did you know about the Lord of Light and all that? About him wanting to take over the world?"

He hesitated and did not respond until the light turned green. "Yes," he said as they pulled away from the minivan.

"Then why did you only want me to learn to defend myself if you knew all of this would happen? Why didn't you tell me about all this before if I can learn to fight this?"

He said nothing for a long time. Emma studied his face. His eyebrows were furrowed, forming deep creases between them. There was swelling under his eyes. His cheeks were sunken and haggard. Her father looked older and, above all, more tired than she had ever seen him before. He breathed deeply several times before replying.

"Maybe I traded the world for my little girl," he said.

They arrived at Jake's apartment building. It was a tall, narrow structure showing signs of age and wear. Jake stood outside the front door, backpack on his shoulders, close to an overflowing garbage can.

As soon as her father parked the car, Emma jumped out. She rushed toward Jake. The boy stepped toward her. Swollen eyes met her own. His shirt had the markings of drying tears.

"I'm sorry," Emma said upon reaching him.

Jake looked down. Tears welled up in his eyes. "I'm all alone now," he said.

Emma embraced him. Though he was bigger and taller, his head slumped onto her shoulder, and then his tears flowed freely.

They drove on to Lucy's house.

Lucy came out holding Sprinkles in one arm and

dragging a small suitcase behind her with the other. The suitcase went in the trunk. Lucy and Sprinkles joined Emma, Jake, and Jingles in the backseat.

"I can't leave him, right?" Lucy said upon entering the car. "I have no idea how long I'll be gone."

"That's good thinking, Lucy," William said.

The humans were silent on the drive back. They stared out the windows at the desolate town. Only Jingles and Sprinkles spoke. Emma eavesdropped on their conversation.

"What sort of thing are you?" Sprinkles said. The cat sat on Lucy's lap and seemed not all too pleased about it.

Jingles responded from Emma's lap. "They call me a jackalope," he said.

"Jackalope," muttered Sprinkles. "I do wonder what you taste like."

Jingles grunted.

"What is happening, anyhow?" Sprinkles said, ignoring the jackalope's grunt. "Why are we aboard this moving prison?"

Jingles grunted again. "It's the end of the world," he said.

"Good," Sprinkles said, though his ears suddenly pinned back against his head. "Finally."

Jingles flopped down on Emma's lap. "Don't worry," he said. "Miss Emma will save us."

They returned home. William Wilkins turned on

the radio to listen for news. They sat in the living room in a dark mood as classical music played on the local station.

Emma watched her father. He sat heavily, hands crossed at his waist, head leaning back on his seat. He closed his eyes.

Will was watching him too. "Dad," he said. "What do we do now?"

William raised his head slowly. He opened his eyes and blinked several times. "Sorry?" he said, frowning.

"Do we just sit here and wait?" Will said. "Shouldn't we pack some things in case Domino says we need to leave?"

"Oh, yes, Will. That's a good idea."

Will stood up. He shot Emma a worried glance, then headed toward his bedroom. William pushed himself up from his seat with some effort.

"Dad, maybe there is more I can do," Emma said.

"Like what?"

"Maybe I should try calling for Domino," she said. "I think I can at least do that much."

He nodded. "Yes, Emma. That's also a good idea. I'll pack some things for you." He turned to Lucy and Jake. "Will you two be okay? Help yourselves to anything you need."

Jake nodded. Lucy smiled weakly. "Thank you, professor," she said. "We'll be okay."

Emma ran to her room and took her flute out from under her bed. She then led Jingles outside to the backyard. A chill breeze enveloped them as they passed through the back door. Sullen clouds obscured the sun.

They went past the deck and onto the grass near the centre of the yard. Emma sat cross-legged and closed her eyes. Jingles climbed up into the nook formed by her legs. He curled up.

"Music is light," Emma said. "Light is music."

She breathed in deeply.

Will finished packing. He closed the overstuffed backpack and placed it on the floor beside his bed. The backpack bulged with clothing. He struggled to think of what he would need. He did not know where they were going or for how long. They would need clothes, yes, but what about food and other necessities? How would everything fit into the trunk of the car? He wanted to talk to his father and ask him what to do. He wanted his father to tell him that he had things figured out, and that he had a plan. His father always figured things out, but today he was not being himself.

He left his bedroom and went down the hallway to the one belonging to his sister. A suitcase lay open on the bed with a few articles of clothing placed carelessly inside.

He looked into his father's office and found him at his computer, reclining back in his chair, re-freshing the City of Saint Martin's website re-peatedly. He took a step into the room, then stopped. What could he say? He did not know how to approach his father, having never seen him like this before.

Will shook his head and decided to check up on Lucy and Jake while he thought about it. A few steps down the hallway took him to the living room.

"So you don't think it will go back to normal?" Jake was saying to Lucy. The boy sat on the floor trying to pet Lucy's cat, but the animal did not seem at all interested.

"It can't, can it?" Lucy said from the couch. "How could it?"

They both looked up at Will as he arrived.

"So what actually will happen?" Jake said.

"Well," Will said. "Dad told you guys about the Lord of Light. He's coming to take over the world."

"But what happens to us? And to my mom and dad?" Jake said.

"I don't know," Will said. "Maybe he'll give back the prisoners. Domino, the faun, said he doesn't know why he's taking them."

"That's the one that Emma's trying to call, right?" Lucy said.

He nodded.

"I want to go see," Jake said.

Will led them to the back of the house. They stepped out onto the deck.

"What is she doing?" Jake said.

"I'm not sure," Will said. "She sits like that sometimes. She explained it to us. She said it's like finding a light inside and using it for magic. I guess she can call Domino by doing that."

"Emma!" Jake called out.

She did not respond. They watched her in silence for a moment. She sat motionless but for the rising and falling of her chest as she breathed in and out. Now and then, the jackalope on her lap would raise his head and twist his ears about, but Emma would not move.

"I wish we could do something," Jake said.

"Well," Lucy said, "they're searching the forest today, right? Maybe they'll find something."

"My dad thinks it will go really bad," Will said. His father had not told him very much about what would happen, but Will had seen the hopelessness in his eyes.

"Hey," Jake said. "Maybe we should go help them. We know all these things they don't. We know there's a tree and the music, and all they have to do is find them."

"That's crazy," Will said. "Dad will never let us. Besides, they're probably already in the forest."

In the yard, Emma raised her arm. She held the flute up in the air for a moment before bringing her arm back down. As far as Will understood, this whole mess had started because Emma had called a creature of the forest by doing something exactly like that. He hoped it did not draw attention to them this time.

"Then we can go to the forest and find someone," Jake said.

"Maybe Jake is right," Lucy said. "It would help

if they knew what they were looking for. I know it sounds crazy, and probably no one will believe it, but it's worth trying, isn't it? We could at least try to convince them. At least we'd be doing something."

"I don't think that's a good idea," Will said. "My dad definitely won't go for it."

Jake sat down. He leaned back against the deck's railing. "I just feel so... useless, you know? There is so much going on, and we're just kids. We tried helping, and it was pointless. I wish I had my dad back. I wish I had my mom back. That's all."

Lucy sat down next to Jake. She put her arm around his shoulders.

"Everything will turn out okay," she said.

"Everyone always says that."

"Listen," Will said. "My dad will figure something out. Don't worry."

Jake stood up suddenly. "Really? It looks to me like he's given up." He clenched his fists. "And Emma's just sitting there doing nothing."

The boy wiped his face with his sleeve, took one last glance at Emma and the jackalope, then hurried back inside.

"Poor kid," Lucy said.

Emma lost track of time.

She did not know how long she had been calling for Domino. There had been no response, even when she had sent the light out into the world using her flute. She lost count of how many times she had tried. She suspected the problem was that she had been trying to be very quiet about it, subdued even with the flute. She did not want to repeat what had happened when she had called Cerynitis.

She opened her eyes. Her vision swam. The world tilted alarmingly. She brought her hands up to her head, palms on her temples, and tried to steady it.

"I think that was too much, Mr Jingles," she said.

The jackalope was fast asleep in her lap.

Emma looked to the sky. The clouds were a violent sea of grey and black. The gloom pressed down on her as it blanketed the world. A wave of nausea ran through her. She closed her eyes and tried to suppress it.

When her stomach settled, she opened her eyes again. The world had some semblance of stability now.

She took Jingles in her arms, careful not to wake him. The jackalope opened his eyes a fraction, clicked his teeth softly, then closed his eyes again. She made her way to the door, stumbling once or twice, and entered a dark, quiet house.

In the living room, she put Jingles down on a couch beside her sleeping brother. Will leaned awkwardly on the armrest, as though he had fallen asleep inadvertently.

She sneaked to her father's office and found him sitting at his computer, slumped in his chair, staring vacantly at his screen.

"Dad?" she whispered. He did not turn. She approached him and touched his shoulder. He trembled slightly, startled.

"Oh, hey," he said and rubbed at his eyes. "Lost track of time."

"Dad, where are Jake and Lucy?"

"What? Aren't they with Will?"

Emma shook her head. William stood up. He picked up his glasses from his desk and put them on. He let out a breath.

They searched the house. Emma went through all the rooms on the main floor. She checked the bathroom. Down into the basement she went. There was nothing there but boxes, old furniture, and Sprinkles, who had climbed inside a basket full of yarn.

"They're not here," she said as she rushed back up the stairs.

She found William standing next to her sleeping brother. He reached out and placed a hand on the boy's shoulder. Will opened his eyes slowly, yawning.

"Oh," he said. "I fell asleep."

"We know you did, silly," Emma said. "Did you see where Jake and Lucy went?"

Will sat up straight, suddenly very awake.

"What? They're not here?"

"I looked everywhere," Emma said.

"They wouldn't sneak out, would they?" Will said. "They were talking about going to the forest to help the search party."

William Wilkins sat down. He looked out the window to the darkening sky. He closed his eyes. His brows furrowed together. He let out a deep sigh.

"Dad?" Emma said.

"I'm so sorry," he said. "But we've lost them too."

"No!" Emma said. "We can't lose them!"

"I'm so sorry," he repeated. "If they've gone into that forest, there's no way to get them back."

He drew her close and embraced her. He pulled her gently onto his lap.

Emma sobbed once, then buried her face into his shoulder.

She thought of how meaningless everything had been. Their search in the forest had amounted to nothing. The promise of magic, the storybook silliness, the foolish notion that she was special. It had all been nonsense. The world was too big. It moved around her, doing what it would, and nothing she could do would change it in the slightest. She had not been able to keep Jake safe.

Here she found herself again in her father's arms, just as always whenever something went wrong. Even now, when she knew a little magic, when she had Jingles as her friend, when she had the great oak on her side, even now she cried on her father's shoulder.

Mr Jingles. The jackalope had said she would save them. How disappointed he would be when the world ended. Then there was Jake. What would Jake think if he knew she had sat on her father's lap while he faced what awaited him in the forest? Jake and Lucy could not use the light. They had not been told they were special. And yet, they were out there trying to help, trying to do what they could.

"No," she said softly.

"Dear?"

She stood up. "No!" she said. Tears streamed down her face. "No, Dad!"

"Emma…"

"We have to help," she said. "Maybe we can't save the world. Maybe we can't stop the minotaur and the Lord of Light and all these bad things, but maybe we can still save Jake and Lucy. We have to try, Dad. If they're still out there, and there's anything we can do, we have to try. I can't just sit here and cry anymore. I can't just give up and cry. We have to try."

William took off his glasses and rubbed at his eyes. He shook his head slowly. He gazed toward the window for a long time. His thoughts seemed far away.

Finally, he turned back to Emma and let out a long, heavy sigh.

CHAPTER THIRTEEN

Battle Song

"You're right," William said.

He stood up. He walked to the window and looked out down the road in the direction of the forest. His shoulders hung heavy. His back slumped forward.

"You're right, Emma," he said, placing a hand on the window and forcing himself upright. "We can't just give up. I'll go look for them. Maybe I can find Domino and he can help."

"I've been trying to call him all afternoon," Emma said. "I'm afraid something might have happened to him."

He smiled weakly. "Well, like you said, I have to try."

Emma nodded. "So do I," she said.

"No, Emma, you stay here," he said and turned toward her brother. "Will, you watch that she goes nowhere. Restrain her if you have to."

He started toward the door, but Emma ran past him and blocked his way. "No, Dad!" she said. "I have to go. You need me. You won't be able to do anything if you can't find Domino. I can call for him from the forest. Maybe if I'm closer, he will be able to hear me. Maybe I can find the oak tree and he can help!"

"I think she's right, Dad," Will said. He stood up and joined Emma. "I've been thinking about it. I don't think all this could have been for nothing. What will you do alone out there? At least Emma can talk to animals and creatures. Who knows what else she can do? Remember the unicorn? When we saw her riding it?"

A long silence followed as William Wilkins regarded his children. He placed a hand on Will's shoulder. He brushed Emma's hair back from her face.

Jingles jumped down from the couch and rushed to stand between the siblings' feet. He raised his antlers high.

"It looks like everyone is against me," William said. He shook his head. A faint smile turned the corners of his lips. He took a step back.

"Will, go to the basement and get us some flashlights. I don't know what else we might need. We don't have any weapons, and it's not like we'd know how to use them, anyway."

"Yes, Dad!" Will said.

Emma ran to her bedroom. She knelt on the ground and took her old, yellow lunch box out from under the bed. A plastic bag held the leftover ribbons from the time they had searched the forest. She took out the longest of these and tied both ends to the lunch box's handle. The lunch box contained all her most valuable possessions, and she did not know what would happen from then on, or where she might end up. She slung the strap over her shoulder and walked out into the hallway.

"What's in there?" Will said when returned to the living room.

"Just knick-knacks, mostly."

"Why are you bringing it?"

"I don't know," she said. "Probably so it gets in the way."

"You're a dork," he said, handing her a flashlight.

William stood by the front door. "Don't forget your jacket," he said. "It's chilly out there. You have that flute?"

Emma waved the instrument about.

He nodded, then turned toward Will. "And where do you think you're going?"

"I'm coming too, of course," Will said. "Someone has to look after Emma while she looks after you."

"Of course. I don't suppose there's any way I can stop you short of tying you up, is there?"

"Nope."

The three Wilkinses and the jackalope passed through the front door and ventured out into the gloom under a darkening sky. Emma zipped up her jacket against the chill. Flashlight in one hand, flute in the other, she followed her father down the driveway and onto Belle Street.

The sound of drums drifted to them from the distance. From the direction of the forest came a muffled, percussive beat, low and ponderous.

"It's the forest," Emma said. "It's not singing anymore. It's doing... that."

"Battle drums," her father said.

Emma shivered.

They continued down the road from island of light to island of light. The street lamps shone weakly, labouring against the gloom.

A blue jay flew before them. It glided and swooped in the air, clicking, whirring, and whining. Three small chickadees sat on a branch nearby. They whistled in unison.

"What is happening?" Will said.

"I think they're cheering," Emma said.

From their right, they heard a terse bark. The beagle Emma and Jingles had met stood on his porch. He marched over toward them. Jingles met him halfway.

"Where do you go?" said the beagle.

"To battle," Jingles said reverentially.

The beagle's tail shot upright. He took a step back and drew himself up. Raising his head high, he let out a great howl.

Jingles galloped back to Emma.

"What is he saying?" Will said.

"Victory," Emma said.

The blue jay led the way to the forest. The chickadees jumped from branch to branch along their way. The beagle howled into the sky until they passed from his sight. Now and then, they saw the gleaming eyes of small critters watching them from the shadows on either side of the street. Through it all, the battle drums continued to pummel.

They reached Lockhart Road. Police cars and unmarked vehicles lined the side of the street. The line started near the intersection and snaked toward the construction site as far as they could see.

The forest's drumming was joined by the sounds of battle. A gunshot burst in the distance. Thunder roared in response. Somewhere in the woods, someone screamed.

They approached the tree line slowly. William switched on his flashlight. He aimed the light into the woods, hesitating. Will did the same.

Emma placed the end of her flute into one of her pockets, the end of her flashlight into the other. She reached out and took her father's hand in hers, then did the same with her brother's.

"Let's go," she said. She pulled them gently forward.

The forest surrounded them.

It happened in an instant, between one step and the next. The forest groaned. The shadows whirled. Browns and reds and yellows blinked by, illuminated by the beams of the flashlights. Above them, glimpsed between the cover of the trees, a black sky roiled furiously. The battle drums redoubled their intensity. They were loud and clear now, booming in their ears.

Emma looked to her family. She saw awe and confusion on their faces. "That happens sometimes," she said, squeezing their hands.

They stood and listened for some time. Gunshots thudded from all around, barely audible above the drumming of the forest. Now and then, they heard peals of thunder from somewhere among the trees.

"We need to find help now," William said, raising his voice above the din. "Do you know how to find Domino, Emma? Or that tree?"

"When I come to the forest," Emma said, "I just walk, and it's like the oak comes to me."

"Then we walk," her father said.

They trudged on through the darkness. They coursed through thick undergrowth, wading through brambles. They circled around trees. At times, the forest barred their way. The brush became impassable, and it forced them to turn from their intended direction. Their path through the woods became labyrinthine, turning them about and soon disorienting them. Jingles was the only one at ease in the forest.

Around them, the battle continued, though the gunshots were ever less frequent. The thunder roared still. It resounded throughout the forest but never from the same direction. Despite the clamour, they saw no one.

"How long have we been walking?" William said.

Emma checked her watch. It was six-fifteen. "I'm not sure. I don't know when we started out."

"Try to keep track of the time. Something seems wrong."

"It feels like we're going in circles," Will said. "Like we're stuck in a maze."

"Emma," her father said. "You said it was like the clearing came to you. This feels like we're being led somewhere. Forcefully."

"It's never been like this, Dad. It was always easy. I don't know what is happening. Maybe I should try calling for Domino?"

"I don't think so," he said. "I don't think we should draw attention to ourselves."

They continued on, plodding through the forest. Emma's arms and legs burned from fighting through the brush. Despite the chill, she wiped sweat from her forehead with the back of her hand. Her heart beat with apprehension, and she tried not to panic. A jolt of anxiety ran through her with every gunshot. The thunder was worse. She had heard it once before in the night. It had signalled the arrival of the minotaur.

She looked to Will. His face, bathed by the light that spilt from his flashlight, was firm with resolve. She looked to her father. He held his flashlight steadily, but his eyes darted everywhere, toward every shadow.

Emma took a deep breath. She wished she could

be like Will and not feel afraid.

On they went as the darkness deepened around them.

In time, they came to a slope. Her watch indicated it was six forty-eight. Their path through the forest had not become any easier, but the sounds of the battle had subsided. The gunfire had gradually died out, and the thunder only came to them infrequently now. The battle drums beat their rhythm still, but they were muted, murmuring in a whisper.

The forest floor rose before them. They clambered up slowly. Emma fell to her knees halfway up. Her flashlight trundled down the hill and disappeared into the bushes below. Will reached for her and took her hand. He helped her along the rest of the way.

They crested the rise and stood in silence at the sight below.

A path opened beneath them. Beyond the path spread a vast glade. It was a roughly circular field with a single tree standing at its centre. The tree was a great oak, broad and tall and ancient. It reached out into the night with contorted branches. A portal of light, nestled in its gnarled trunk, bathed the clearing with its silver light. It was not Emma's tree, but its twin.

Surrounding the tree, in disorderly rows, sat dozens of human prisoners. Those nearest the oak were dressed in plain clothes: a mixture of jeans and t-shirts, dress pants and buttoned shirts, track suits, dresses, leather jackets, and even pyjamas. Their ages were just as varied. Teenagers and seniors huddled next to the middle-aged. Toward the back of the group, the prisoners were predominantly dressed in uniforms bearing the insignia of the Saint Martin Police Service.

Great, hulking beasts tread heavily among the humans. Trolls, orcs, and ogres patrolled around the perimeter of the clearing and marched between the rows. Centaurs ran down any who, roused by a surge of courage, tried to escape. Harpies flew above the crowd, shrieking now and again at those below.

Emma hardly noticed it all. She stood transfixed, wide eyes locked on the creature standing next to the portal. The minotaur stood taller than any of the monsters roaming the clearing. His tapered black horns glistened in the silver light. Blazing eyes bathed his bull's face in blood red resplendence. He stood seething with power, the perverse mass of his body swelling with rage, watching as trolls snatched up humans and threw them into the opening of the portal, one by one.

"Oh my god," William said in a hoarse whisper. "Turn off the lights. We need to get down from here and hide."

But it was too late. A harpy swooped in the air and wailed, sounding the alarm. The trolls nearest the harpy stopped in their tracks.

"Dad," Will said hurriedly, pointing, "it's Lucy."

Emma squinted and saw her. Lucy sat, legs

sprawled, near the back of a row of prisoners, disparate in her dark jeans and jacket among the uniformed officers.

Emma sprang forward. Her father grabbed her arm, stopping her in her tracks.

"Emma," he said. "We have to run."

"They've already spotted us, Dad," she said. "We have to run, but we have to bring Lucy with us. And maybe when they chase us, other people can escape too."

The fingers around her arm relaxed. She shook free and ran down the path. Jingles galloped next to her. Will and her father were not far behind.

"Lucy!" Emma called out, loud as the harpy. The girl in the glade looked up. She rose to her feet unsteadily.

"Run, Lucy!"

Lucy stumbled toward her. She swayed for a moment before steadying herself and lurching forward into a precarious trot.

All eyes turned toward them, the two girls running toward each other on the forest path.

A harpy flew overhead and shrieked at them. A troll lumbered behind Lucy, closing the distance between them quickly with long, rumbling strides.

Emma's gaze darted about beyond the troll, desperately scanning the huddled humans for a sign of Jake. More of the creatures hulked toward the path from the clearing, obscuring her view.

Lucy faltered. She lurched forward and landed hard on hands and knees. Emma reached her side.

Lucy's jacket was bloody and dirty. There was a gash across her forehead. Thin streaks of blood ran down her face.

Emma winced. "We have to run, Lucy," she said. The troll was nearly upon them. "Where's Jake?"

Lucy looked up. Tears and blood blended together on her cheeks. "Gone," she said. "Into the tree. He struggled, so they threw him in."

Emma's world spun. She found herself down on the ground next to Lucy somehow, suddenly nauseous and spent, feeling as though something inside her had snapped in half.

Will arrived beside them. William ran past and stood between them and the charging troll. He raised his arms as though intending to fight.

Jingles rushed to stand next to William. The jackalope reared his antlers defiantly.

The troll lunged at them.

Like a blur, the faun emerged from the shadows of the forest. In one fluid motion, he squatted on his goat's legs then dove forcefully into the troll, using his horns to batter the monster's ribcage. The force of the blow sent them both spiralling into a tree. Domino rolled away and settled into a crouch. The troll sprawled on the ground, limp and immobile.

"You should not be here," Domino said. "Run."

He rushed to Emma's side. His arms wrapped around her and lifted her off the ground. The faun's skin was startlingly sleek and warm.

Enraged grunts and growls drew her attention.

She stared toward the clearing over the faun's shoulders. Several more creatures—orcs, ogres, and trolls—trampled toward them.

"Where?" William said. He and Will helped Lucy stand.

"Only one hope," Domino said. "Quickly—"

Suddenly, a white light filled the sky. With the light came a booming voice. "Titanius!" the voice roared.

All the creatures in the path looked up to the sky in awe, halting their advance.

But soon, the voice faded, and the light went out.

"What was that?" Emma said, wide-eyed.

"I do not know," Domino said. "Maybe... no, there's no time. We must run."

Thunder erupted. A deafening rumble shook the earth. The creatures turned aside to flank the path. The minotaur had come forth from the clearing. He stood resplendent in the light from the portal.

Emma looked into the monster's eyes. Crimson fire blazed and whirled around them. Black orbs of contempt regarded her back. A cold trail of fear rooted itself in her stomach and spread throughout her body like a spider web.

Domino screamed, "Run!"

He plunged into the darkness of the forest with Emma still in his arms. She glanced back to see the rest of the group scramble into the shadows, stumbling in the dark. The two beams of their flashlights lurched desperately behind the faun's trail.

"They can't see us!" Emma said. In response,

Domino's flute flared with golden light. The shadows retreated.

They ran. Domino sped through the forest. Trees flashed by on either side. The autumn colours of their leaves merged together rainbow-like above them. Jingles galloped beside the faun, keeping pace with him. The rest of the group lagged behind, losing ground.

"Slow down!" she said.

"No," said the faun. "You must escape. I can help you flee, at least."

"We needed your help. I called you, but you didn't come."

"Domino is not my true name, girl." He bared his teeth as his face contorted into a grimace.

Thunder roared. Not far away, from the direction they had come, a scarlet glow bathed the trees crimson. The light raced toward them, accompanied by heavy, hammering footfalls.

"Minotaur is coming," Domino said.

Emma's family, unable to keep up with the faun, fell behind. Lucy teetered alarmingly, swaying as her legs lurched forward in wild strides.

"They will get caught!" Emma said. "Put me down!"

The faun did not speak. He ran on, chased by thunder.

The forest shimmered ahead of them. Silver rivulets of light flowed among the trees. They rippled, expanded. The faun rushed straight into the light.

They broke into a clearing. Emma understood.

The great oak who had gifted her the flute stood at the glade's centre. A portal of light glimmered beneath its branches, nestled in its trunk, undulating in time with a soft melody that emanated from the tree. They could escape the minotaur through the portal.

"We have to wait for them!"

Domino did not slow down. Emma writhed in his arms. "Stop!" she yelled as the faun dashed toward the oak. She kicked at him and shoved hard with her arms, breaking free. She hit the ground hard. Her momentum sent her rolling. The jackalope was at her side immediately.

The faun approached.

"We have to wait," Emma said. She stood up unsteadily.

Domino sighed. He turned toward the forest. "As you wish," he said.

Emma held her breath. She stared into the woods, searching for some sign of Lucy and her family. She could see the red glow of the minotaur's eyes. She could hear the rumble of his strides as they beat the ground.

A moment later, Will arrived at the clearing. He was followed by Lucy and, bringing up the rear, William Wilkins. All three gasped for breath. Lucy seemed on the verge of losing consciousness.

There was no time to waste. "Hurry!" Emma said. "Into the light!"

Thunder roared.

In an instant, the minotaur was upon them. The

monstrous creature burst into the clearing. Before any of them could react, he clamped his hand around William's leg and lifted him into the air. Will and Lucy backed away in terror.

The monster held Emma's father aloft like a trophy. He twisted his wrist viciously, breaking the leg with ease. William Wilkins screamed.

"Dad!" Emma wailed. She rushed toward him. Domino's hands dug into her arms and kept her in place.

The minotaur slammed William to the ground. Her father writhed in agony, clutching at his leg.

Emma kicked at the faun. "Let me go!" she screamed.

"I will stay and help," Domino said. "You must go." He picked her up roughly.

The minotaur raised his fist.

Domino threw her into the portal, as he had done once before. Time slowed down. She saw the faun dart toward the monster. She saw her father raise his arms to shield himself.

She saw lightning as it raced through the forest toward the clearing.

Emma was then ripped apart by the light of the portal.

CHAPTER FOURTEEN

The Wizard and the Lightning

E mma floated in light. She was in a space without bounds speckled with stars. A wind enveloped her and swept away the fragments of her body, carrying them away like leaves in autumn. Left behind was a spark, and the spark was Emma.

She watched the parts of herself glide away and dissolve into nothingness. The spark that remained quivered in place, flickered unsteadily. She wanted to run away but could not. She fluttered left, right, rebounded back to where she had started. Panic stabbed at her.

A star came near. Slowly, it floated toward Emma, seemingly expanding as it approached. It came to rest in front of her and sent undulating waves of warmth toward her, a warmth she had felt before on the bark of a tree.

Emma knew then that the star was the great oak in the forest. She had been here once before but had forgotten.

The star glimmered. Briefly, he shone brighter. The flash of light passed through Emma and brought with it a single note. Light and music together filled the spark she had become.

Again the star glowed.

All around Emma, the field of stars drew closer, mimicking the oak, each point of light sending forth a flash of light and a note of music. They waited. As far as she could sense, in every direction, the stars waited.

Emma remembered her lessons. Domino had taught her how to empty herself, how to push away the universe and embrace the light. But here, she was the light. Her true self was not her body, which had floated away, but a spark of light inside a field of stars.

Emma sparkled.

But the stars waited still. Something was missing. She had used her spark before to speak, to shout, but the stars had done something else. They had sung. But Emma had no voice. How could she sing?

As though sensing the question, the great oak glimmered again. This time, he sent forth not a brief flash, but a sustained shimmer, showing her what she needed to see. The light was imbued with a faint shade of yellow.

Music is light, Domino had said, and light is music.

Emma searched her entire being. She was a spark, but the spark was made of infinite parts. It was a rainbow woven together and entangled with itself. She had spoken and shouted with her entirety, never realizing her pieces were infinite.

She swam the sea of colour, seeking the one to match that of the oak. She picked at the fabric of her being for the right thread. Upon finding it, she pulled, plucking it above the ocean of colour. It became a shroud upon her being.

Emma sparkled. She was light together with music. The field of stars sparkled in return. From every direction, they shone and sang their single note in unison.

The great oak changed then. His hue shifted from yellow to blue. Emma swam the ocean of colour once again and matched that of the star. A different note emanated from her spark. Like a game, they changed colour and sang different notes.

Now the oak moved. He swerved and spun. Emma followed. A twist and a turn. Emma gave chase.

If she had had her body then, she would have giggled in delight.

They whirled and spun among the stars, all the while shifting colours and stringing notes together. The rest of the stars followed from a distance, spectators to the chase, their colours also changing until they were as varied as their number.

As they danced among the ever-changing star field, twisting and turning and whirling together, the notes they produced formed a song, and the song was a story.

The great oak, the star, told the story. Emma listened and duplicated it, learning the tree's dance and his music.

The song, the story, began with the name of the tree and his twin, for they had been the first. Their names were a verse, twin pieces of melody forever intertwined in harmony, but they had once been known as Life and Knowledge to some inhabitants of the earth. They were not bound to a single place, but could exist wherever there was need.

Once, they had roamed the world and sowed the seeds of the trees. When they had finished, the forests had stretched from sea to sea on a planet of green and blue.

Nothing disturbed the peace of the world but the wind that coursed among the trees and swayed their crowns. For an age, the world remained so.

But one day, a concept appeared. It was a new thing unlike any the trees had ever envisioned. Among their forests, there walked a creature who moved about by his own will, one who affected the world in the ways of his choosing. The creature was the Lord of Light.

The trees saw the concept and imagined more like him. They sang the new concepts into being.

In this way, elves and dwarves came to be, along with unicorns, minotaurs, gnomes and goblins, dragons, and all the creatures and beasts that ever walked the earth or crawled upon it. But the Lord of Light was the first, and he ruled the world for an age.

Among all creation, one creature resembled the Lord of Light most closely. Humans were, in imitation of him, more distant from the embrace of the trees than the rest, treasuring instead their independence and autonomy. They spread out to all corners of the earth.

In time, the Lord of Light came upon a human woman whom he took as his wife. The woman became the night and gained power over it. She was called the Queen of Darkness.

The Lord of Light and his queen ruled over creation for an age, and all was in harmony.

But there came a day when she fell in love with a human. She betrayed the Lord of Light. He, heartbroken, fled the earth. Gathering all his power, he created a new world. A new place he called the World of Light. Forlorn and spent, he hid. Weak and wearied, he rested.

A new age began. When they learnt that the Lord of Light had vanished, the humans, unrestrained by his power, ran amok. They brought down trees and built houses. They killed the creatures that inhabited the forests and ate them. They wore their furs and made trinkets from their bones.

The Queen of Darkness saw the destruction

and interfered. They killed her, revelling as they burned her body in a great pyre.

Many of the world's creatures went into hiding. Others followed the Lord of Light into his new world. In time, they were not remembered on Earth but for the myths and legends that remained behind.

In his world, the Lord of Light waited. He waited for the day when his heart would be mended, his power restored.

He vowed to return one day. He vowed to retake the earth, and to punish the humans who ravaged it.

Thus the song ended.

Emma's heart was heavy. The world was fading. The light around her dimmed. As the stars went out, she tried desperately to cling to the memory of the song.

A fading melody slipped away into the night. On a cool wind it drifted, flowing over an old wooden fence and across an empty field. The melody glided above the rippling water of a lake, then disappeared into the darkness.

Emma stood on a porch in front of an old house. A bare bulb hung from a beam above and spilt its light onto worn steps. She looked out into the night, longing after the vanishing melody. She did not know where she was, or how she had arrived there, but she knew the melody was important somehow.

Clack-clack.

She searched her memory. Faint traces of places and faces were all that remained, but they were mere impressions seen through a thick fog.

Clack-clack.

In the fog of her mind she glimpsed the trace of a tree, tall, old, and dignified. A tree surrounded by stars. It was there, from the tree and the stars, that the song originated. She needed to find her way back to that place. Urgency stabbed at her. Something had happened. There was little time to waste. She had to—

Clack-clack-clack-clack.

"Okay, okay!" she said, turning and shaking her head. "What?"

"Hello, Emma," said a voice. To her right, in the shadows, sat an old man, *clack-clack*ing away on a rocking chair. He closed a tattered old book and rested it on his belly.

"Hello, mister," Emma said. "My name is Emma? I'm sorry. I was just thinking."

The old man adjusted his thick-rimmed glasses and stood up. He stepped forward into the light. A ring of grey hair crowned his head.

"It's all right," he said. "Thinking is good. I do it myself quite often, though maybe not often enough. How are you feeling, Emma?"

"I'm not sure," she said. "I don't remember anything. Do you know how I got here?"

"Yes, I do," he said.

"Can you tell me?"

"You just appeared there," he said, snapping his fingers. "Just like that. It's an old trick. Old as the world." He smiled and tucked his book under his arm. The wooden boards under his feet groaned as he made his way to the door of the old house. Tired hinges groaned loudly as he pushed the door open. "Come on inside, Emma. We need to have a little talk now."

She hesitated. The feeling of urgency tugged at her. There was somewhere she had to be, something she had to do.

"I think I need to go," she said. "I need to go... somewhere, I think."

"Don't you worry about that," the old man said. "There's no rush. Come on now."

Emma could think of nothing else to do. The man knew her name, so maybe he could explain to her where she was, and what she was doing there. He had a kind face, besides.

She stepped into the house and promptly sneezed. A thick layer of dust covered old, shabby furniture. Musty books lay scattered about the place. Great cobwebs covered every dark corner. A plump spider stared at her from the largest web.

"Pardon the mess," the old man said. "I've been out and about for a very long time doing this and that. You know how it goes." He motioned to a chair next to a rickety table and Emma sat down. From a grimy refrigerator, he took out a plastic pitcher. He poured a clear liquid into a glass.

"Drink this. It will help you remember."

Emma took the glass and eyed the liquid inside it suspiciously. She shook it and watched the clear liquid slosh around. "What is it? A magic potion? A memory serum?"

"It's water."

"Oh."

She shrugged and brought the glass to her lips. The water was cool. It tasted delicious. She chugged it all down greedily.

"More please, Mr Clarence."

The old man's eyes twinkled. He refilled her glass, grinning all the while.

"Thank you, Mr Clarence," she said.

"You're welcome, Emma," he said, still grinning. "It will only be a few moments now. The teleportation, or whatever you want to call it, can really confuse the mind. Luckily, it only lasts for a little while. Unless you travel very great distances, that is. You'd have to travel much farther than you have for the effect to be more than a little temporary memory loss."

"Is that how I got here?" she said. "I remember lots of lights and a tree."

"You went through a portal in a tree and found yourself here." He frowned and pursed his lips. "It sounds quite silly when you say it out loud, doesn't it? Singing trees and portals and all that." He shook his head. His grin returned. "But never mind," he said. "That's not important now. As I was saying, the tree sent you where you needed to go, and so you came here to talk to me. I've been waiting for you."

"But who are you?"

The old man sighed, and a faraway look took over his features. "A good wizard," he said after a moment. "You need one in every good story. As for my name, I've been called many things—some not very endearing, that's true. But you know who I am, Emma. You have been using my name for a little while now."

"Mr Clarence!" Emma said. Her eyes opened wide. It was as though remembering his name had let open a dam. Memory came flooding back. She remembered the clearing in the forest. She remembered the minotaur towering over her father.

Her chair scraped the floor as she stood up. "I have to go!" she said. Cold panic gripped her heart. "Where am I? What can I do? Help me, Mr Clarence!"

"Settle down, Emma," he said.

"My dad is in trouble and it's all my fault!" she said. "I started all this! Then I convinced him to go to the forest, and the minotaur got them. There's this monster in the forest, Mr Clarence. We went to look for Jake. He got them, and it's all my fault. We need to help them!"

"Emma," Mr Clarence said. "You're very far away from the forest now. Too far to do anything useful at the moment. Please calm down and listen to me. I have to tell you something very important. Take another drink of water and try to calm down. This will only take a moment."

She took the glass from the table with shaking hands.

"This is very important, Emma," he said. "You are about to go on a very big adventure. Enormous. First, you need to go back to that clearing and defeat Minotaur. But that is only the beginning. The Lord of Light is coming, Emma. It's up to you to stop him."

Emma shook her head. She gripped the table with both hands and sat back down. "What can I do, Mr Clarence? I don't even know where to start. How can I do any of these things? I'm just a kid. Why is everyone telling me all these things about being the only one that can stop him? I don't understand."

"That's another thing I have to tell you," he said. "All you have to do is listen. You haven't been listening, even though the key to everything has been there all along. You see, the trees are the best teachers when it comes to the old tricks." He winked.

"I still don't understand. Listen to what?"

"I'm sorry, Emma," he said. "I'm very used to speaking in riddles, you see. It's almost tradition for my kind. Just promise me you'll listen." He pushed his chair back and stood up. "But now it's time for you to go back to that forest and face Minotaur."

"I can't do it, Mr Clarence," she said. "I don't know what to do or where to go. I don't even know where

I am. How can I fight him?"

"Remember your favourite book," he said. He held up his old tattered volume. "It's all right if you're afraid, or feel that you can't do it. But if you go ahead and do it anyway then, you see, that is something very special indeed. Sometimes we all just need a little push out the door. That's part of the reason I'm here."

"But they're all gone," she said. "My dad, Will, Lucy. Mr Jingles, too."

The old man reached toward her. She took his hand. He led her to the front door and out into the night.

"Emma," he said, "you just have to listen. Promise me you'll listen."

She nodded.

"Good," he said. "Now, let's take care of that awful Minotaur, why don't we? Do you remember the first time you went through a portal? Where did it send you?"

"To a hospital."

"Ah, yes, but *when* did it send you."

"It was the next morning," she said.

He nodded. "What time is it, Emma? Let's have a look at your funny little watch."

"It's six fifty-three," she said. The grey mouse was grinning and giving a thumbs-up. "Mr Clarence, is it still the same day?"

He laughed a deep hearty laugh that made Emma giggle along despite everything. "It is indeed," he said. "There is still time, but you are so very far away, Emma. What can you possibly do?"

"How far, Mr Clarence?"

"Very, very far."

Emma let go of his hand. She had last checked the time when they had crested the hill and come upon the clearing that held the hostages. The time had been six forty-eight. Then they had seen Lucy, fought the troll, and run through the forest. There was still time, but how could she get there if they were so far away?

"Lightning!" she said. "The lightning!"

"Yes!" he said. His eyes twinkled.

Emma jumped from the porch. She ran into the night, through an open gate, onto the empty field. "Thank you, Mr Clarence!" she yelled, turning back to see the old man wave goodbye.

One breath was all it took to find her spark. Somehow, she knew she *was* the spark. She raised her flute high over her head. The spark blazed through her.

"Titanius!" she cried out. Her voice erupted into the world along with her light.

Lightning shattered the darkness across the lake. Water heaved and surged in great torrents as the unicorn soared above it. Titanius burst onto the field, flickers of lightning clinging to his mane still.

He bowed. "Princess," he said, kneeling before her.

She climbed onto his back. Her spark danced inside of her as she spoke. "We need to save my family," she said. "I need you to take me to Mr Oak's clearing."

The world became a blur as the unicorn took her into the night.

George Clarence watched the girl and the unicorn fade into the distance in a flash of light. He brought his hand up and scratched at the fringe of grey hair on his head.

"I hope I haven't sent you to your death," he said. He let out a long sigh. "And I hope we can meet again, Emma Wilkins, Princess of Light."

The old man chuckled to himself, turned, and went back into his house.

The girl and the unicorn were lightning. The darkness parted before them as they streaked through the night. Arcing tendrils of electricity surrounded them and trailed in their wake, crackling like autumn leaves caught underfoot.

They bolted over the countryside. The land tumbled beneath them. Rolling pastures gave way to winding hills shrouded in fog. They cut through the gloom and surged over the hills, picking up speed all the while.

A river flashed beneath the unicorn's hooves. Cold jets of water sprouted into the night air.

A dark forest loomed before them. They snaked through the trees, passing through a glade and skirting the waters of a miry pond.

Over a flat country they flew. The landscape, featureless at first, quickly became a grillwork of roads and highways spiderwebbing in every direction.

A pinpoint on the horizon flared up and became a great city. Skyscrapers stood tall and bright against the black sky like monuments to light. Vehicles scurried about their bases, zipping along wide roads in all directions. The lightning raced among them, dashing through the streets, darting around cars, and leaping over intersections. Wherever it passed, all eyes turned toward the flash of light. Those eyes saw lightning, and in its midst they saw a great unicorn ridden by an armoured princess. Her breastplate gleamed in the night. In her right hand, she held a sword. A shield hung from her shoulder at her side. They saw her for only an instant, but the afterimage of the princess riding into battle burned in their minds for long after.

A harbour sprawled at one end of the city. The lightning streaked through it and sprung into a vast lake. Torrents of water burgeoned in its wake as the surface of the lake parted before it.

The lightning tore through the night as its destination rose in the distance. Across the lake, huddled in darkness, lay the City of Saint Martin, desolate and hushed, as though holding its breath.

The world was a blur. Emma held on to Titanius as they flew over the dark surface of the lake. Electricity crackled around her. Jets of cold water sprayed in all directions. Directly ahead, the black

sky pressed down heavily on the growing silhouette that was the City of Saint Martin.

With a great leap, Titanius shot clear of the water
and landed on the shore. The thin strip of sand on
the waterfront did not slow his pace. They raced
down the empty streets of the city. Houses flashed
by on either side, little more than ghostly grey
streaks in the night.

Emma's heart raced along with the unicorn. They
were near now, almost back to the forest and the
clearing, almost back to her family and the minotaur. She did not know what she was supposed to
do once she arrived, but at least she had Titanius
with her now. The thought gave her some measure
of comfort.

In a blink, they were back inside Glenridge Forest. Titanius flew among the trees. They were
a bolt of lightning dashing through a maze of
brown, red, and gold.

The unicorn did not slow down as they approached the clearing. Instead, it was as though
the world came to an abrupt halt around them.
They arrived at the oak's glade a mere instant after
Emma had left it.

The portal closed. The tree's melody persisted,
though now it was only a quiet hush. The golden
light of the faun's flute and the red glow of the
monster's eyes were the only lights that remained.
Those eyes turned toward Emma and Titanius.
They widened in surprise.

The minotaur drew himself up and turned to

face the new arrivals. Will and Lucy rushed forward and pulled William away. Her father groaned as they dragged him back along the forest floor. The creature ignored them, his full attention now on the girl and the unicorn.

The minotaur spoke. His voice, like a great tremor of the earth, roared through the clearing and out into the woods. "Horse," he said, addressing Titanius, "when did your kind bear a rider last?"

"Not since the War of Light," Titanius said, "when we stood for the queen and failed to protect her. When we carried her to each corner of the earth, and still it was not enough to save her."

"Do you mean to save this one then?"

"I don't need to," Titanius said.

The golden light behind the minotaur shifted. The monster twisted and snatched something out of the air. When he turned back, he held Domino by the head in one giant hand. The faun had crept up to the minotaur and had tried to leap at him in attack.

"I have had just about enough of you," the minotaur said. He closed his great fist around the faun's horns, crushing them. Domino howled in pain. The beast tossed him aside. The faun's body struck the ground. He lay still. His flute rolled away from limp fingers. Its light went out.

The minotaur's eyes turned back toward Emma. Blazing furnaces bore into her, drawing a shudder from deep within her chest. She glanced around the clearing, avoiding the monster's gaze, and could not keep herself from trembling. Will and Lucy crouched beside her father. Jingles skittered around Domino's motionless form.

"Girl." The minotaur's voice battered her hearing and drove waves of fear through her. "You have no one left to defend you. The horse will not interfere in this. You should not have returned." He shifted his gaze to the unicorn. "Stand aside, Titanius."

The unicorn turned an eye toward Emma. "I am sorry, princess," he said, "but he is right. I cannot interfere. Not this time." With those words, Titanius knelt and bowed his head, urging her to dismount. Emma held onto his mane with a trembling fist for a long moment before descending from his back.

Titanius stood and moved aside, leaving her alone to face the minotaur.

Emma clutched her flute in trembling hands, feeling smaller than she ever had before. Now that she was away from the unicorn's warmth, the cool night air gripped her viciously. She gathered her arms to her body and held her jacket close as a shiver ran through her. She took an unsteady step forward, head bowed to avoid the minotaur's gaze.

Suddenly, a great shudder shook through the minotaur, and a rumbling roar, like a mountain toppling down, escaped his throat. Emma stopped in her tracks and stared wide-eyed at the monster. It took her a moment to realize he was laughing at her.

When the rumbling died out, the minotaur spoke again. "What will you do now, princess?" He spat out the last word.

The monster took two steps forward and stood before Emma, towering over her. The girl and the monster faced each other under the black sky. Emma fought the urge to run away. She held her ground, though she could not stop her trembling.

The minotaur crouched until his head was nearly level with Emma's. Thick knots of muscle writhed under his skin. His mouth curled back, and his jaws swung open. The minotaur roared. The fire in his eyes blazed with fury.

"Nothing to say?" bellowed the minotaur. "Will you not speak, princess? Even now as your world is ending?"

"I am not a princess," Emma said, forcing the words out past the cold knot of fear in her chest. Her voice quivered and sounded small to her ears. "I haven't said anything because I've been listening."

From the periphery of her vision, she saw the faun stir. He raised his head from the ground. Broken stumps protruded from his skull. Nearby, Will was helping her father as he struggled to stand. William's face was a mask of pain.

Emma raised her arm to the side. She held up her palm. There was nothing the faun or her family could do now.

Domino continued to rise but settled into a crouch. Her father stood still, leaning heavily on

Will's shoulder. Lucy wavered next to them, unsteady on her feet.

Only Jingles ignored her signal. The jackalope left Domino's side. He bounded over and sat down halfway between her and the faun. Little antlers rose as he looked at Emma, hope and adoration written plainly in his eyes.

"Miss Emma," Jingles said, "you're glowing."

Emma smiled at the jackalope. A faint glimmer surrounded her.

"I've been listening, Jingles," she said. "Will you sing with me?"

It had been there all along from the very beginning, from the moment the great oak had called her to the forest the first time. Now, as she listened, she heard the same melody coming from the old tree. It was a melody she knew, one she had been taught but had forgotten. Even now, she remembered only the tree and the stars. But she knew the song, and she knew her own part. It was a song of power and sorrow.

With a deep breath, she reached inside herself to the spark within. But it was not just a spark. It was an ocean of colour, and each colour was itself an ocean of music. She dove into that ocean and, following the great oak's lead, she sang her own part in harmony. The spark inside her blazed into a great flame that enveloped her.

The minotaur took a step back, eyes wide. His nostrils flared, and his chest heaved, as he realized what was happening. He raised his arm and made a great fist. He dashed forward to strike at Emma.

But it was too late.

Emma guided the flame to the flute in her hand. A blaze of light shone forth and struck the minotaur. The monster toppled backward and fell, crashing to the ground. He roared in anger. Spittle flew from his lips, and hatred burned in his eyes.

The minotaur scrambled to his feet. He lunged at Emma yet again. She knocked him aside with a wave of her hand.

A third time the minotaur attacked. And a third time he was bashed to the ground.

Battered now, he gripped the earth in impotent fury. His chest heaved as he let out a series of ragged growls. His fiery gaze shot around the clearing.

The minotaur scrambled to his feet. He did not attack this time, but turned toward the forest.

The monster fled, but Emma's song was a song for many voices.

She raised her arm, flute held high. The light and the music flew to the sky and lit up the night. From all around the clearing, new voices joined the song, coming together to create a symphony.

The forest came to life. All around them, the woods groaned. The ground heaved beneath their feet. The crowns of the trees swayed and drifted.

Where the minotaur ran, the forest drew close together. The earth surged and rolled in waves, and the trees sailed through it like ships in the ocean. They barred the monster's way and herded him in a different direction.

The minotaur's face contorted painfully. He ran away into the woods, crashing into trees and bounding off them all the while, forced to run along a path the trees created.

Emma felt a nudge at her side. Titanius now stood beside her. He bowed. Emma jumped on his back and glanced around the glade.

Will and Lucy, wide-eyed, disbelief plain on their faces, held her father between them as they approached.

Emma smiled, suddenly holding back tears.

Lucy, blood still dripping slowly from the gash on her forehead, smiled and waved weakly with her free hand.

Her brother only frowned.

Her father smiled, but there were tears in his eyes. He held her gaze for a long while, then sighed heavily and bowed his head. He understood.

Jingles stood near Titanius' hoof.

"Promise me you'll take care of them," Emma said to the jackalope.

The jackalope grunted and reared his antlers. "I promise, Miss Emma," he said, "but hurry back."

Next, she looked to Domino. He crouched on the ground still. The faun nodded gravely.

"Time to go, Titanius," Emma said.

The unicorn sped into the forest along the path the trees had made, trees each adorned with a colourful ribbon tied neatly onto the lowest of their branches.

The forest turned against the monsters. Throughout the woods, the earth heaved and surged like a great beast, long asleep, finally waking up. The trees hunted. They roamed the forest, herding all the creatures under the minotaur's command. Centaurs and trolls, orcs and ogres, and even the harpies, they all fled from the trees, funnelled by their movement into a clearing in the woods.

The prisoners in the glade huddled close together as the forest roiled around them. They had seen the tower of light as it had risen to the sky. They had felt the earth tremble. They watched now as the trees shepherded the creatures back into the clearing. From all around the tree line, they came. Running wild-eyed, the monsters scrambled past each other, pushing and shoving, all trying to reach the portal in the centre of the clearing.

From the woods came a vicious growl. A path had formed at one end of the glade. It was flanked on either side by neat rows of trees bearing strips of cloth on their lowest branches. All eyes turned toward the new gap in the tree line.

The minotaur emerged, snarling, eyes darting everywhere in desperation.

Behind the monster, a bright light spilt out from under the cover of the trees. Into the clearing came forth a great unicorn. Atop the unicorn sat a rider: a small girl bathed in light. A silver circlet, sparkling like her breastplate, rested on her brow.

A shield hung at her side. In her hand, she held a bright sword. The unicorn reared as they came to a halt. The battle princess lifted the sword. It blazed in the night.

The unicorn's hooves thudded back to the ground. The rider pointed her sword at the minotaur.

"Minotaur," she said. Her voice rang clear throughout the glade. "Leave this world!"

The minotaur cowered, scrambling backward. He turned toward the portal in the tree and ran. There was no thunder this time, and the fire in his eyes had been quenched.

Emma watched as the last of the creatures ran into the portal. A great shudder ran through the forest one last time, shaking the ground beneath Titanius' hooves, and then all was quiet. The symphony had reached its conclusion.

In the silence that followed, Emma let out a long breath. Suddenly she was exhausted. Heavy eyelids threatened to close on their own as though she had not slept in days. The edges of her vision blurred. Her head hung heavy. She held on to Titanius' mane to keep herself from falling over. It would be easy to let go, climb down, curl up on the forest floor, and fall sleep. But it was not over yet.

With a heavy sigh, she straightened her back and lifted her head.

It was then she realized that every eye in the

clearing was on her. Dozens of faces, each bearing an expression of astonishment and elation, were turned in her direction. Someone cheered. Someone laughed. Then the clearing erupted into a hail of applause.

Emma blushed. For a moment, bashfulness supplanted exhaustion. She peeked about for a good hiding place but decided it would be ridiculous if she crawled behind a rock.

"I don't know what to do," she whispered to Titanius.

"Wave to them," said the unicorn.

She tried to steady her nerves then raised her arm and waved.

The crowd's cheering redoubled.

Titanius stamped a hoof. "Enjoy this," he said, "as I carry you forth for the last time." He turned toward the shimmering portal and set off at a walk.

Around the periphery of the clearing, Emma could see the gleam of small eyes appear in pairs as the critters of the forest returned. From the branches of the trees and the forest floor below, the animals watched as she rode the unicorn toward the oak. Emma could not be sure, but she thought she could hear the quiet goodbyes of the creatures of the woods.

Titanius halted before the portal in the tree. He bowed. Emma dismounted on teetering legs.

"Thank you, Titanius," she said.

"It has been my honour, princess. But you must hurry. The portal might not remain open for long."

"I didn't even get to say goodbye," she said. She thought of her father and his broken leg, Lucy with the gash in her forehead, Domino and his shattered horns. Only Jingles and Will had escaped unscathed. They all would have each other, at least. She would have no one.

Emma did not know what awaited her on the other side of the portal. She did not know when, or if, she would return and see her family and friends again. But she had to go, for Jake and the rest of the prisoners, and she had to do it alone.

Tears pooled in her eyes once more. This time, she let them run free. She turned toward the portal and took a step forward.

A hand wrapped around hers. She nearly jumped at the touch. She turned and saw Will. He was gasping for breath.

"How?" she said.

"I ran after you," he said.

"But why, Will? I have to go."

"I know," he said, "and, of course, I'm coming with you."

Emma shook her head. "We don't know what's out there. I don't know how long I'll be away."

"I know," he said. "But I'll be there with you."

Emma looked up at her older brother. She saw the determination in his eyes and knew he would not be deterred. She was scared to go on alone, but Will was never scared. No matter what they found on the other side, if she had her brother with her, then she would be a little less frightened.

"Okay, Will," she said. "Let's go."

They turned toward the portal, hand in hand, and together they stepped into another world.

EPILOGUE

The Prophecy

L ike a song in the wind, the tale drifted out to the world. It started its journey in a dark glade deep inside Glenridge Forest. Those who had been there to witness the story carried it with them into the City of Saint Martin.

From there, told and retold, the tale transformed and grew wings of its own. Farther and farther, the tale flew, reshaping itself into the form given to it by the voice of the teller. The story morphed and shifted, ever molding itself to the temperament of the land beneath it.

The tale reached every corner of the world. To some, it was only a children's bedtime story. But others, in times to come, would find in it solace and truth.

It was the story of the captives in the woods, and the demons who surrounded them. It was the story of the Princess of Light, who arrived on a bolt of lightning, fought the monsters, and banished them.

She left this world, it was said, to embark on a quest to save those who were lost. But the day would arrive when she would come back.

During the darkest hour, in the time of greatest need, the Princess of Light would return.

The Story Continues In

EMMA
and the
PRINCE OF SHADOWS

Visit jonherrera.ca for news and information.

Printed in Great Britain
by Amazon

76461420R00144